The Butterflies' Story

1.

As I lay on my back looking up at the ceiling of the cabin, I saw what I had never seen before, ET's sister, or at least a good likeness of her.

I had not been here long, just long enough to feel the chill seeping into my bones and a sense of strange distancing that comes when your brain has been otherwise engaged.

ET`s sister pestered me. I should have noticed her before; I wasn't sure if she was laughing at me or just looking on perplexed.

I came to this cabin every morning seeking peace and solitude; I should have seen her before. Was she here yesterday?

As I lay there contemplating, I thought perhaps she could be my friend. She might not be as scary as she looked; in fact through my life I had discovered that quite often people were not what they seemed.

I remembered that tall dark-haired man that I caught a fleeting glance of out of the car window.

I had fantasied about him for the whole car journey and looked for him again every time I went past the bend in the road that wound over the downs into the small coastal town where I worked. He appeared to me to be the man that would have completely mirrored me, perfect, singularly good-looking, a great sense of humour and a love and understanding of the great outdoors. But he wasn't real I never saw him again, was she real?

I decided that I needed to move back into the day that was wakening slowly. The chill mist that had initially greeted me was evaporating never to return in the exact same way. As I moved through the cobwebs that were littering the grass, I became engrossed in observing the minutia of life. Was I a giant to these small scuttling creatures and were they giants to the pollen and dust particles that they moved through? These were unanswerable questions that the universe wasn't going to tell me.

Three weeks ago when I looked across the expanse between my house and the nearest village that had tethered itself to the hillside on the opposite side of the valley, the grass had been brown and you could imagine it crunching under your feet as you walked. Now it was just showing green and the sheep and cows looked more relaxed as they ate.

I wondered as I walked back up the hill if the wine I had drunk last night had befuddled me, maybe drinking a whole bottle of the pinot last night, and all previous nights for the last month was rotting my brain, making it hard to distinguish between fact and fiction. I would need to get a grip on a sort of reality if I were ever going to fulfil my dream of developing a vineyard here. Ever since I had moved here I had wanted to grow things, anything really, the miracle that is planting a small dark seed, watering it and then watching it slowly emerge from the soil had always held me in awe, but now, now I was contemplating bigger things.

2.

Running my hand through my unruly auburn hair, I fondly

remembered Horace, the old man whom I had bought this little homestead from in what seemed like eons ago now – was it really only six months? He had proudly shown me the blocks of gnarled old pinot noir vines planted on the sunny north-facing slope of the hill – Amelia's Hill he had called it, after the devoted wife whom had left him bereft following septicemia from a small cut sustained whilst opening a can of dog food, the recipient of which now sat patiently at his masters feet, looking up with loyal eyes. The old man looked distant, as if he were seeing the vines in a different time, young and vibrant like the image of the young woman which rested in a small silver frame in pride of place on the dusty mantelpiece in the living room of the cabin.

The Pharaoh family who owned the neighbouring land had offered old Horace a pittance for his homestead, but I had paid him the full asking price, much to the annoyance of old Walter Pharaoh, the overbearing patriarch of the clan.

Horace had lived and loved here for over 80 years, and had struggled on, trying to scratch a living from the land he had given his lifeblood to. But now, having no heirs to help him, he could no longer hold back the devouring march of nature, and it was time to sell up and settle down in a small bungalow on the coast with his dog.

I had the inheritance from my mother's estate, and if I was careful, I should be able to give my vineyard plans my best shot, mindful though of the adage - to make a small fortune in wine, you must start with a large one!

It was a poignant day when Horace handed over the keys to me, but there was also an optimism that I hadn't noticed in the old man before.

"Look after them," he had said, nodding towards Amelia's Hill.

"I will," I responded eagerly, giving him such a tight hug that for a moment I thought I could feel some sort of energy transferring through his tatty hand-knitted Fair Isle jumper which filled me with an invigorating warmth.

"I'll bring you a bottle of my first vintage when it's ready."

Horace nodded benevolently and drove off towards the coast, his dog sitting by his side in his beat-up van. As I turned to survey my new acquisition, I had seen old Walter Pharaoh leaning over the gate glaring at me with such a look of hatred in his ice blue eyes that it had made my blood run cold.

3.

My befuddled brain took me back to this encounter as I returned to my house.

I was made of sterner stuff than to be scared off and I had vowed at that moment to make friends with Walter and show him what a lone woman could do, if given a chance. My mental health training had taught me that most people had reasons to behave in the odd ways that they did and that if I got to know him, I might be able to take some steps to understanding him.

I still didn't know whether it was just Walter who felt aggrieved or if it was his whole family. I didn't even know who else was living with him on the property. The old building looked foreboding, a bit mysterious and not at all welcoming.

The driveway to the house was shielded from view with big metal gates, but there often seemed to be vehicles coming and going which indicated that there were more people than just him living there.

For a short while I mulled over what opportunities might be available to me to contrive a social gathering that he couldn't avoid coming to, but then my head became distracted by the hangover that I was trying to fight, and I decided that I needed to eat something and put off the tricky question of how to placate Walter.

I wandered into my tiny scullery kitchen; I have no idea what attracted me to it. I think I had a romantic idea that the small space would seem intimate and endearing. Just now as I fought my way through the mess trying to cook something before I felt too ill, I longed for my old kitchen with its sleek units and clean surfaces. There was no going back now after my marriage to the wonderful cheating Frank failed, the house had to be sold and with it my dream kitchen.

My good friend Victoria was due to visit me next week. She was going to be my adviser. She authored articles for The Guardian reviewing wine productions and innovations in practice.

I needed to tidy the house and garden and review my ideas for regenerating the vineyard before she arrived.

4.

The light coming in through the small sash window created rusty patterns on the old Formica worktop. The colours reminded me of old Horace's dog. A complete ailurophile myself, Victoria wasn't the only female showing up next week. Isis, the gorgeous black cat that I had rescued the year before I moved here had spent her customary time in quarantine and was arriving on the same day as my dear friend. Isis, always a good judge of character had taken an instant dislike to Frank! Well it would be all girls together now, and an all-female household – for a while at least, whilst my fractured heart mended.

My thoughts turned to Victoria – she was a real good time girl, and that's when I had the idea of throwing a party, to welcome my friend and introduce her to those I had made in my short time here. After all, I had never had a housewarming, and the Pharaohs' were not the only people I didn't really know locally. This would be the perfect opportunity to meet Walter in a congenial setting and find out who else lived with him in that big old house. He couldn't really decline a housewarming invitation - could he?

I had always loved cooking and entertaining, and now plans of what I was going to cook filled me with happiness. I would make a list, and then drive into town to get the ingredients. But this would have to wait until I had spring-cleaned the kitchen!

A couple of hours later I was driving down the winding road to the coastal town. It was a beautiful journey, with rolling hills flanking much of the route, and flowers carpeting the sides of the roads with their myriad colours.

Pulling into a parking space outside the grocery store, glancing in my interior mirror as I did so, I realised that I had been so engrossed in my party plans that I had left the house without bothering to run a brush through my hair, and that had a mind of its own at the best of times. Fumbling in the glove compartment for a comb, my fingers closed around a metal case – it was my signature coral lipstick that I thought I had lost in the move! Using the mirror to apply a slick, I noticed a tall dark-haired man walking along the pavement on the far side of the road. He looked vaguely familiar, and my heart nearly missed a beat as I realised it was the same man I had glimpsed through my car window on that particular bend of the same road I had just driven – the same man I had continued to fantasize about ever since!

In my confusion the lipstick broke against the corner of my mouth, covering my right cheek with a bright slash of coral. By the time I had hastily cleaned myself up he had gone.

But before my clumsy accident, I had managed to see that he was at least 6ft tall, with a strong handsome profile, dressed casually in well-cut jeans and an open necked pale blue shirt. He carried himself with that confident bearing of a man that knew his purpose in life.

Feeling foolish, I collected everything I needed from the store, with the checkout girl giving me a quizzical look – checking my face again once back in the safety of my car I saw that I hadn't fully succeeded in removing all the lipstick from face. Thoroughly embarrassed now I drove home, trying to peer into every shop and down every street as I left the town, hoping to locate my handsome mystery man. As I passed Gardner Street, I noticed Walter Pharaoh going into the bank, which made my heart quicken for a different reason.

5.

On my drive home my mind wandered, and it was hard to concentrate on my driving. Ever since I had divorced Frank I had stayed away from men. I wanted now to focus on a different type of passion.

I had been fascinated by the process of creating an intriguing wine ever since Victoria had explained to me the intricacies of the craft, and her passion had transferred to me. She had supported me through the rough times with Frank, her honest and open style of communication had really helped. No bull shitting from her. If she thought I was making a fool of myself she told me and suggested ways of being more assertive. There was the time that Frank insisted that he would be taking all our music collection as part of the divorce settlement, stating that I didn't need it as I could get it all online now. Some of those CD's we had danced to together night after night. It was a sensual ritual that bound us together with our bodies swaying in sync, mimicking and exaggerating the passion that we felt. I wanted those CD's. However, Victoria pointed out that when I was at work doing my night or evening shifts, he was dancing to our CD's sensually with Stella, the woman from the post office. Why did I want to keep them with those memories?

I couldn't really explain. I think I held on to a belief that he had loved me, and I was special even in the light of such treachery.

I wanted to repay Victoria in some way for her support and thought that she might be interested in coming into business with me. I had heard from an acquaintance that there was recently an upsurge of vermouth making in Spain. Could we produce this here? I had no idea what it would entail but knew that Victoria would know. And with her skills and my money perhaps we could start making the best vermouth to go with the local gin.

Gin is my second passion in life, the subtleties that good gin makers get into their spirits is so wonderful. The perfume and textures that are woven through a good distillation can send you into a heavenly place.

I once cycled with a bottle of gin for 40 kilometres on the Isle of Jura having sampled the local gin there. It was produced in what was essentially a shed, having been set up by three women who grew or collected all the botanicals locally. The intense pleasure of drinking that gin was one of the highlights of my life. There was nothing better after a long days cycling.

Apart from the vermouth musing, my mind was wandering to "the man." Oh, my goodness what had come over me? Here I was vowing to never go near another man, and I was fantasising about the feel of his hand on my skin and the laughter we would have together. This had to stop. I did not need to be distracted by such intrusive thoughts. ET's sister and a handsome man all in a few days; what was wrong with my brain?

On my return home I emptied the car of the shopping and slowly found homes for all my fresh produce in my cool larder, as yet I had not purchased a refrigerator. This was an ancient skill of storing food that I was gradually adjusting to. The lack of a refrigerator would prove a challenge when I hosted the housewarming party. I did not want to give anyone food poisoning, not even Walter.

6.

I had just finished putting the drizzle through the proverbial lemon drizzle cake when I heard that oh so familiar step on the tarmac, and then Victoria burst through the door, pulling her suitcase behind her, laden with bags and parcels. Rushing forward we hugged in that familiar way that only good old friends who haven't seen each other for a while can.

"God I've missed you," she trilled, "especially your wonderful cooking," nosing the air in the direction of the kitchen. "I can smell you've made my favourite."

A good three hours later, sitting side by side on the chintz sofa, drinking black coffee and scoffing the newly baked cake with a contented Isis between us [the cat had arrived in her crate in the last hour and had made herself at home immediately], I had told Victoria everything that had happened to me since I moved here, all about my job, my plans for making vermouth, the enmity I felt from Walter, and the plans for the housewarming party. Well, almost everything, the only thing I left out was about the mystery man.

"Well," said Victoria speculatively, "Vermouth is an aromatised fortified wine, so if you want to make your own vermouth, you have first to make your own wine." It's having quite a renaissance now in Blighty with some wineries making their own versions.

"Let's go and take a look at your vines," she announced, standing up immediately.

"Don't you want to take a nap first?" I asked, "Don't you feel jet lagged?"

Laughing with that gay abandon I loved about her, she shot me a look as if to say I should know better.

"There's no time like the present," she said with authority, and with that we were both heading out the door and over to Amelia's Hill.

Victoria whistled appreciatively through her teeth when she saw the vines. Crouching down and taking a stem between her thumb and forefinger she glanced up, her large grey eyes filled with wonder.

"These must have been planted in the late 70's, did Horace make wine from them, and have you tried any of it?"

Her questions were tumbling out almost incoherently now – she was clearly excited by what she saw.

As we made our way back down to the house I explained that Horace had been reluctant to talk about the vines, all I knew was that he had once made wine and won a few medals locally apparently, but that information had come from one of my work colleagues. I did know though, from his parting shot, that he had wanted me to look after them, and I had promised to bring him a bottle of my first vintage.

Victoria listened to all this intently, and then declared mischievously,

"Well, the sun is over the yard arm now, so let's go and sample some of that famous local gin you've been telling me about."

I laughed my agreement and we continued our way back arm in arm. As we rounded the corner to the house, Victoria noticed the old shed which stood facing the veggie patch.

"What's in there?" she said inquisitively.

"Haven't looked yet, just haven't had the time, been meaning to get around to it," I replied.

"Be a wonderful place for a still," she chirruped as we bounded through the door of the house.

7.

The smell of the lemon drizzle cake still hung in the air, the sharp but honeyed fragrance was a reminder of the gin and tonic we were about to try. I had made my own tonic water sourcing illegally the cinchona bark for the quinine kick, and then collecting lemon grass from the local market and, lemons and oranges for their peel from the trees in my garden. I had been experimenting with which other botanicals to use, and in this batch had added cardamom, allspice and dried lavender. I thought it tasted wonderful with my local gin, having just the right amount of flavours not to overwhelm the gin and not too sweet. The evocative smell took me to a paradise long forgotten when I was naively looking forward to a life married to Frank.

I went to my newly fashioned kitchen cupboard hastily made from old packing cases and retrieved my best crystal water glasses that had been my mums' pride and joy. The ice part of this cocktail was a challenge without a fridge or freezer, so I had purchased ice from the supermarket and kept it in my old chilly bin on the back deck out of the sun. I put the glasses on the table in front of Victoria and hopped off around to the back deck to retrieve the ice. I was excited by the prospect of setting the perfect gin and tonic in front of her and us sitting down to watch the sun dip behind the distant hills. I loved the way that, even long after the sun was heading to another time zone, the sky continued to throw a spectacular light display, the black shape of the mountain silhouetted by crimson fading up through pink to the eventual inky blackness of the night sky. I wanted this backdrop to accompany our first evening together as we reminded ourselves of why we were friends, sharing memories and forging new plans.

I opened the heavy dark green chilly bin and screamed. Nestled inside on top of the ice was a dead rat with its head severed, eyes bulging, and the words "Moneyed Bitch" written on a piece of paper tied around its bloated body. I screamed again, initially not being able to take in what I was seeing just knowing that it was of evil portends. I didn't hear Victoria arrive by my side; I just felt a tug as she grabbed me by my blue silk scarf pulling me out into the garden where I fell into a heap amidst the nasturtiums that were growing wild on the bank. The smell of the crushed foliage surrounded me in a pungent haze that invaded my hysteria like a thick cloak.

I continued to cry not being able to catch my breath my whole being overwhelmed; I was shaking and stammering incoherent words.

Victoria pulled me to my feet and dragged me back across the garden around to the front door where we nearly fell over a man standing on the path that led from the track into the house. I was so distracted that I didn't even notice that it was, the man, the tall dark stranger.

8.

"What's happened?" he said with sincere concern, "I was passing your drive on my way to see my uncle when I heard screaming." Still unable to catch my breath Victoria replied guardedly, "Some sick bastards left a decapitated rat with a malicious note on top of the ice in the chilly bin."

Before I knew what was happening, the man had followed us into the house, and was now asking if there was anything he could do. Beginning to calm a little now, I noticed how the light emphasised the green glints in his hazel eyes.

"Excuse me," Victoria barked, putting a protective arm around my quivering shoulders, "but who the hell are you?"

"I'm Matt Pharaoh," he said softly, not looking at Victoria, but directing his gaze and answer to me.

I was now sitting on the sofa, and my brainpower was returning, trying to make sense of the situation.

Although the colouring was different, there was no mistaking the likeness Matt bore to Walter Pharaoh. He had said he was on his way to see his uncle, and the road past my drive led directly to the Pharaoh homestead.

Victoria had taken Matt outside to show him the evidence. He disposed of the rodent's body and now they had returned to the living room with one siting either side of me on the sofa. Victoria had poured three generous G&T's sans ice.

"We need these," she said reassuringly.

As I gulped down the lukewarm liquid, the familiar aromatic taste was a soothing influence on my frayed nerves. I noticed how Isis rubbed herself against Matt's legs and he made no attempt to shoo her way.

"We need to call the police," Matt said.

"No," I said forcefully, "I don't want whoever did this to think that I am some weak woman who can be frightened off by one dead rat. I mean to find out who, and what's behind all this, and put a clear message out there that I am staying put. I have plans for this place, and nobody, nobody is going to stop me from realising those!"

An hour later I had told Matt exactly what my plans were, and he had nodded encouragingly. Isis had nonchalantly moved up onto his lap and he was stroking the thick black fur absent-mindedly.

I also told him about the menacing looks his uncle had been giving me. I thought too that Walter was constantly watching me. I hadn't voiced this to Victoria, but I did feel that although he wasn't always visible, he was following my every move. So, I figured now was a good time to sound out my concerns.

Matt looked uneasy.

"Walters a contrary old man for sure," he said, "but I can't really believe he could do this," gesturing to the note that now rested on the coffee table, a corner of the buff coloured paper tinged a vibrant red.

"Well, perhaps you can tell me why he gives me these hostile looks," I said defensively. "I'm not imagining it."

Matt looked apprehensive.

"I'll talk to him," he said gently, "but I really can't see that this is his handiwork," waving his hand in the direction of the note. "So, what are you going to do now?"

"As I told you," I said emphatically, "I'm going to carry on with my plans, and the next item on the agenda is my housewarming party."

We were both standing up now, and I glanced up at him with my azure eyes, aware of the closeness of his athletic body, breathing in the faint piney scent of his aftershave.

"You and your uncle are invited," I carried on breezily. "I'll drop off invitations in a couple of days. Can I give yours to Walter?"

Matt nodded his agreement.

"Oh, and by the way, does anyone else live with your uncle whom I need to include? I've seen a few cars coming and going."

"Yes," answered Matt, "Auntie Clare, Walter's wife and their son, my cousin Simon. You might also want to invite Simon's girlfriend Sarah.

I'll be off then," he said, I thought a little reluctantly. He was still holding my gaze and continued to do so as he pressed a card into my hand.

"My number, in case you think of anything else and would like to talk things through. Otherwise, I look forward to seeing you again at your party." And with that he was out the door heading for his car. My eyes followed him as he went, but when he tuned and caught my look I hastily turned back to Victoria like a shy schoolgirl.

"More gin?" she said brandishing the gin bottle in one hand the tonic in the other.

9.

Victoria slept in the bed with me that night; I was too scared to be on my own. My imagination was running riot and the gin, although at first settling, had now made me fractious and on edge as if I was waiting for a fight. Victoria put a bolster between us in my big old-fashioned bed. It had come with the house and the springs squeaked when you rolled over. That didn't matter too much when you were on your own but was disconcerting when trying to sleep with someone else. I had often wondered if any children had been conceived in it and what secrets it might hold.

At 2am having initially fallen into a deep alcohol induced sleep I awoke with a start, my heart pounding. I felt sick and had a headache coming from the top of my scalp and running down into my neck, all my nerves felt as if they were being pulled taught like a guitar string about to ping. As quietly as I could I rolled out of bed, found my old tatty dressing gown on the back of the door and felt my way to the top of the stairs. My spatial awareness is not good, and having once wet myself in the bedroom of a strange house because I couldn't find my way out being too scared of falling down the stairs, I am now incredibly careful. I feel the rough wall of the passage and remember how many steps to the top of the stairs. Once there I count the ten steps to the first landing and then the six down to the stone floor of the hall. Then I can safely turn on the kitchen light.

As I made my way to the turn in the stairs, I could see out through the narrow hall window across to Walter's House. There was still a light on and as I started to move into the hall, I thought I saw the lights of a car heading out of his drive, but when I looked up again, they had gone. I felt too ill to wonder what was going on and thanked my lucky stars that I had brought some of my strong pain killers with me from England.

I took two with a large glass of warm water which made me retch and settled myself on the sofa, trying to lie so that my head didn't pound quite so much.

Through the waves of nausea my mind kept wandering to Matt. I had been too engrossed in the moment earlier to think clearly, but now as I lay here it came to me that it was a bit odd that he heard me screaming from his car. Was it too convenient; was he too nice, too caring? But then I thought Isis liked him. I wasn't capable of coherent thought and soon fell into a fitful sleep scrunched up on the sofa.

I dreamt that my head was wedged in a wooden gate and I couldn't get it out. I tried moving it in all directions and it just caught me tighter and tighter. I thought that I would die. I then became aware that I wasn't wearing any clothes and in the field on the other side of the gate there were hundreds of rats laughing at me. I could hear their shrill menacing squeals and see their sharp pointed teeth. I started to wonder how I had got here without clothes. The rats kept on laughing but they didn't come close. I thought they feared me because I was naked. Part of me thought this must be a dream, and I know if it's a dream you can think yourself out of it.

I thought of Matt coming to help me. I willed him to come, but then out of the corner of my vision I saw Walter coming towards me. I screamed and screamed but nothing came out of my mouth, my throat was tight and I could not make the noise I wanted. Now hands were gripping me, shaking me. I tried to fight but I couldn't move.

"Jenny, Jenny wake up it's a dream."

This sound came through to me, filtered as if through a dense calico curtain, but suddenly I was awake and staring into Victoria's eyes.

10.

"Oh, thank goodness," I stuttered, grabbing Victoria close. "It felt so real, so terrifyingly real!"

"I'll make coffee," she said softly.

I dutifully followed her into the kitchen, leaving the living room where the remnants of last night's gin session remained on the coffee table, the aromatic smell still lending a faint fragrance to the morning air. I noticed that the note had gone.

I watched Victoria as she proficiently made coffee, grinding the fresh beans in my old, well-used, but much-loved grinder, and made toast, thickly spreading it with the pale butter I bought from Mason's Farm, topping it with the marmalade I had made from the oranges growing in my garden.

After settling me on the sofa again she brought the whole lot through on a tray, nudging the glasses and bottles out of the way and placed it in front of me on the coffee table.

"Where's the," I said, waving my hand in front of me. I couldn't bring myself to say the words, but Victoria knew what I meant.

"I put it in that drawer over there before I went up last night," she said kindly.

"Now, tell me about your dream, or rather nightmare."

Re-telling the images, drinking the strong coffee, and eating the warm toast with melting butter and rich sharp-sweet marmalade filling my mouth, normality slowly returned to my disconcerted brain, and I was able to give a wry smile when Victoria said,

"You always did have such vivid dreams Jenny. Go up and get dressed," she continued, "I'll clear up here, and then we can discuss our next move." I duly obeyed.

Talking through last night's events cemented my intentions to carry on with the life I planned to make for myself here, in this stunningly beautifully remote part of the world that had completely seduced me since I first arrived.

When I came down I voiced to Victoria my query about how Matt could have heard my screams, but she reassured me that he had been driving a convertible car – the top was down. In all the confusion and terror of the situation I hadn't noticed.

"And you didn't clock that when you watched him leaving?" Victoria asked with a playful smile twitching at the corner of her mouth. I felt myself blush and gave her a light-handed slap on the arm.

"So, party and vermouth it is then, let's go and have a look in that old shed," she responded.

Out in the cool air I was relieved to see there were no laughing rats to be seen, and Walter's house looked benign nestling in its hollow across the field. The wood of the old shed glowed warmly in the early morning light, and seemed to beckon, inviting us to open its ancient door, worn smooth by so many other people opening it over the silent-footed years.

I hesitated, staring at the metal pewter-coloured latch, but Victoria just opened it with one deft flick of her thumb, and before I could procrastinate further, she had linked my arm and pulled me inside with her.

As our eyes adjusted to the murky light, I noticed an old pull cord light switch hanging down just inside the door. Reaching out to tug it I was aware that my hand passed through a filigree of spider's webs. I didn't mention this to Victoria, she hated spiders. With a flash the old bulb burst into light, illuminating the interior of the shed with what was still a bright beam.

We just stood there, with gaping mouths and wide eyes – turning towards each other, azure met grey.

The whole place was kitted out as a winery. There was a de-stemmer crusher machine, a wine press, two tanks - one stainless steel and one wooden, pumping apparatus, and a selection of oak barrels of varying sizes. In fact, all the equipment you would need to make wine.

We were both scrambling about now, me marvelling, and Victoria examining everything. Uttering a squeal of excitement, I saw her scamper over to the far right-hand corner of the shed. Her voice came breathily,

"I hope this is what I think it is." After a few moments of scurrying around Victoria emerged holding a dilapidated wooden crate, her treacle-coloured hair anointed with cobwebs.

"What's that?" I asked incredulously.

"Wine," she called in a triumphant voice. "Must be some of the wine Horace made over the years. And there are loads more like this!"

I gestured at her hair. With a shriek Victoria understood what this meant and shoved the crate into my arms as she sped off towards the house. She was a courageous woman, but her courage stopped short at spiders.

As I made my way to the front door, I was aware of a shrill ringing. Entering the house, Victoria, who had regained her usual composure, was talking on the phone, which she now waved at me.

"Who is it?" I asked, setting the crate down carefully on the floor.

"Matt," she replied simply.

11.

"What does he want?" I mouthed; my mind was all engrossed in the wine and I didn't want to talk to Matt now.

"Oh, Matt, Jenny has just come in, I will pass her the phone so that you can talk to her directly," Victoria said grinning from ear to ear ignoring my frantic waves of admonishment.

I took the phone glaring at her.

"Hi Matt, what can I do to help?" I managed to ask.

"Well Jenny, I thought I would see how you were this morning after the drama of last night."

"I'm fine thanks," I lied not wanting to discuss how wretched I felt with a stranger.

"And how did you get my phone number?" Despite my frazzled state I knew I had not given it to him.

"Victoria gave me one of your work cards on my way out of your house last night."

I looked daggers at Victoria.

"It's not one I share widely," I retorted. I knew that my answers were short, sharp and grumpy, but I didn't really know why; I didn't feel like trusting anyone now.

Aware that I was being rude to someone who had helped me I quickly added,

"Please don't share it with anyone else; we are fine and thank you for your assistance last night. I am just trying to forget about it and start to make plans for the party. I'll contact you in a couple of days when I have some details."

"OK," he said, "I am here for three days and then heading back up to Auckland, you have my number and don't hesitate to ring."

I put the phone down feeling childish and sensing Victoria's eyes boring into the back of my head.

"OK, OK," I said "I know I was rude, let's not talk about it. Let's get back to planning how to progress with the wine making and party arrangements."

Victoria was sensitive enough to let it drop for now, but I knew she would wheedle it out of me later. Why couldn't I be civil to Matt?

Victoria suggested that at lunch time we open one of the bottles of Horace's wine so that we could assess what had been produced here in the past. She said that this was a good starting point for deciding what would need doing with the vines and the winery.

We spent the rest of the morning clearing out the shed to see what was still potentially functioning and what else we would need to purchase. Luckily, I am not scared of spiders so went in ahead with my long-handled broom and a vacuum cleaner.

I don't normally like to kill spiders as I think they do a lot of good in catching flies and other less useful insects. We do not have any deadly spiders here in New Zealand, and apart from the occasional white-tailed spider which gives a nip that can fester, there is nothing to worry about. But fears are fears and it was full of cobwebs which wouldn't be particularly good to get in the wine.

My fear was wasps so I hoped that Victoria would reciprocate in the role of exterminator later in the year when they became more prevalent.

It became hot as the morning progressed and I was looking forward to lunch. I asked Victoria if she would mind going up to the house and open the wine whilst I finished cleaning the first side of the shed.

"There are a selection of cheeses and hot smoked salmon in the pantry. The salmon will need eating today. It is smoked locally, and I only bought it yesterday, but it won't last long in this heat," I instructed her.

"You will find the bread in there somewhere as well. Take it all out onto the table under the shade of the fig tree and I will join you shortly."

Victoria left with anticipation in her step. I think she was pleased to be away from the cobwebs.

I turned back to the job in hand assured that it wouldn't take me more than ten minutes to make this side of the building look presentable. I was lost in thought wondering what the wine would be like and guessing we might not get much done this afternoon after the wine tasting when suddenly I froze. I could hear a tapping noise; my nerves were on edge. I stood still, attached to the ground through my feet as if I was tethered by a huge anchor chain to the very bowels of the earth. My breath came in fast rasping gasps. I could feel

the vibrations of it through my skin, and felt if I moved I would pass out. I could hear Victoria calling my name but couldn't respond; every one of my senses was telling me I was in danger. Victoria's voice got louder and louder.
"Jenny lunch is ready, leave what you are doing, we can finish it later."
Still I did not move. I was sure if I moved whatever it was that was making that noise would get me.

12
My brain was in overdrive. I knew that in Maori culture ghosts and spirits were considered a taboo subject, but I had learnt a lot from Anahera, the beautiful Maori solicitor who had helped me acquire my property, and I had become fascinated by the proud indigenous people whose country I had chosen to make my own. This was a spiritual place and being here had awakened the spiritual side of me that I always knew I possessed. Anahera had told me that when Maori die, their body needs to be returned to their family as soon as possible. It is believed that if certain rituals fail to be conducted, the family of the deceased are likely to face stress and unhappiness, and if the spirits are not satisfied, they may choose to take someone else. The Maori also think that the spirits of the dead watch over the living and warn of danger. I truly thought I was in danger right now from some malevolent force.
"Where are you?" Victoria's familiar voice broke through my reverie, then she also stopped dead in her tracks – she could hear it too.
"What is that noise?" she murmured, dropping her voice to a whisper.

"I, I don't know," I stammered, "but it is really scarring me."

The tapping was coming from the opposite corner to where the wine had been stashed.

"I'm going over to take a look," said Victoria, the slight break in her voice belying her fear, but before I could protest, she was stealthily inching her way over to the far left-hand corner of the shed where the walls converged.

After what seemed like eons, Victoria's voice came reassuringly from the gloom.

"It's all right Jenny, come and take a look."

"Are, are you sure?" I stammered; the tapping was still clearly audible.

"Yes, really, come and see for yourself."

Standing now by Victoria's side I peered down to what she was indicating. Victoria continued,

"All the clearing up we've been doing must have disturbed these cables, and the wind coming through that crack in the old wood there has made this bundle of wires here continually beat against that old iron tank."

Feeling rather foolish now, I bent down to tug the offending cables away from the tank to stop their incessant percussion. In doing so I dislodged it and fell backwards, landing on the dusty floor of the shed with a thump. Sheer relief made hysteria turn to hysterics now, and as Victoria helped me to my feet, we were both laughing uncontrollably.

"Come on," I breathed out between giggles, "let's go and have lunch, we certainly deserve some wine now."

Bending down to re-tie a shoe lace which had come loose during my inelegant fall, I noticed that displacing the tank had revealed an opening directly underneath.

Victoria had noticed it now too, and between us we manoeuvred the rusty old tank out of the way to get a better look at what lay under it. There was a hole roughly two feet wide, and in it lay a wooden box.

"You get it out Jenny," Victoria shrilled, a little nervously. I knew she was worried about any eight-legged visitors, so I reached down and with both hands, sliding one beneath, and resting the other on top of the box, brought it clear of its hiding place in one adept move. The box was reddish brown in colour and oval in shape with every surface ornately carved. It was exquisitely beautiful inlaid here and there with pāua shell. It was locked.

We were sitting under the fig tree now: Victoria having set up lunch before coming to find me in the shed.

The box sat between us accusingly on the outdoor table, like it was daring us to open it.

"Let's leave that till later," Victoria said assuredly, lifting up the box and placing it on the ground at the base of the decade's old fig tree. I knew she was anxious to try the wine, and I would have to find some tool to break into the box anyway. I didn't want to damage its intricate patterns.

Victoria explained that she had found an array of vintages, and in order to assess the wine properly, we would need to do a vertical tasting – tasting multiple vintages to see how subtly or dramatically the wine has changed over the years, starting with the youngest first.

She had lined up six bottles in the order of tasting, with wine glasses, paper and pens to make notes, and two jugs. One jug was filled with water and the other would act as a spittoon she said. Seeing my look of protestation Victoria explained that this was like a scientific experiment and should be taken seriously if we were to truly assess what we had here and determine what the vines up on Amelia's Hill were capable of. We would assess each wine systematically, both individually making our own notes without conferring on each wine, describing its appearance, nose, palate, and our conclusions. She had prepared sheets of paper for us, one for each wine, with these categories marked out, with each one further divided into various sub-sections.

As I reached out to help myself to a slice of hot smoked salmon, Victoria tapped my hand away from the food like an authoritative school mistress.

"Lunch after tasting, we don't want to spoil our palates," she said in a voice that broke no challenge.

And so, we began …

13.

For all my love of wine I was a novice at wine tasting, and was apprehensive about how I would complete this task. I thought about it for a bit and watched what Victoria was doing. I took a sip from my first glass and swilled it around my mouth as I had seen Victoria do.

I couldn't really tell what I was tasting, but it was quite nice. Oh, how my mum hated that descriptor. "Nice," she would say, "that tells me nothing." I used to think, "Yes it does. It tells you it's not nasty."

I noted on my paper, deep red colour, smells of cinnamon and blackberries, a bit thin. I swallowed without thinking and looked across at Victoria to see if she had noticed. Thankfully she was fully engrossed, her eyes screwed tight swishing wine around her mouth and slurping, which was a very strange sight. I started to giggle and she opened her eyes.

"What?" she said, "What are you giggling at?" I tried not to laugh more but failed.

"You," I said. "You look like a witch tasting a special brew."

"Well it is a bit like that," she opined. "Can't you take this seriously at all?"

Duly chastised I attempted to control my features and get on with the task. I was after all very hungry and the sooner we did the sooner we could start on the food in front of us. I was beginning to wish that I had not asked Victoria to lay the food out; it was attracting the flies and wasps.

I kept on swallowing rather than spiting, force of habit I suppose. The more I swallowed the hungrier and tipsier I became.

Thankfully, Victoria finished her sampling smiled very broadly and said, 'Well what do you think?''

"I think it's very good," I slurred.

"Good," she retorted. "What kind of assessment is that? You will be telling me it's nice in a minute." She reached across to take my scribbled paper, but I pulled it away from her before she had a chance to reach it. I didn't think "nice, nice and very nice," would go down too well.

"Let us eat," I said. "And whilst we are doing that you can talk me through your assessment of the wine."

I reached for some salmon and this time thankfully my hand didn't get swiped away. Victoria on the other hand gazed into the far distance and said,

"I think we are on to a winner here, brilliant just brilliant," and then used lots of terminology for the wine that I really didn't follow.

She now took a large purposeful mouth full of the oldest wine and thankfully swallowed it, slowly, but she did swallow.

Victoria spent the next hour enthusiastically telling me what we could do and how fantastic it would be. The more she drank, the more she waved her arms and the more purposeful and extravagant she became in her proposals. I didn't follow everything she suggested as my head got befuddled through the wine and the heat of the sun shining through the fig leaves.

As the afternoon progressed Victoria's plans became even more elaborate. My eyes started to glaze over, and I was about to doze when I heard the familiar drone of a wasp. I squawked and jumped up, not looking down as I was intent on escaping from the stripy winged creature and stumbled over the box, falling to the grass and rolling a little way down the bank into the mānuka bushes; they were very prickly.

The pain in my foot and the prickles took my mind off the wasp for a minute. It was Victoria's turn to laugh now.

I sprawled on the grass cursing my clumsiness. I decided that the box had to be opened but I wondered how I was going to open it without damaging it. I staggered in an un-ladylike fashion to my feet and as I gained a nearly vertical posture, I heard a toot on a horn. I turned my head and saw Matt waving as he drove back to Walter's house and hoped he hadn't witnessed my rolling about on the ground or heard my cursing. I made my way to gather "box getting into implements." As I meandered back under the weight of the tool bag plus various kitchen implements, I could hear

Victoria shouting from under the fig tree.

"Was that Matt? I wonder where he's been."

14.

"Probably going up to see his family, he did say that he would speak to Walter about the filthy looks he's been giving me. I wonder if he's done that," I said pensively.

"Why don't you give him a ring," Victoria offered.

"I'll leave it for a bit, see if he contacts me," I responded breezily.

"Besides got more pressing things to see to," I said, entering the house with the box under my arm, and setting it down on the coffee table.

"First though, I need a nap."

"Good idea," replied Victoria. I returned the remnants of the food to the safety of the cold larder, whilst Victoria set all the half-imbibed wine bottles and tasting paraphernalia on the coffee table, ringing the box like a protective corral, and with that we both collapsed onto the sofa and fell into contented wine-induced slumbers.

It was a good few hours later when I stirred, thankful that my head was clear. I got up to make some coffee, leaving the still sleeping Victoria gracelessly draped across the sofa, a barely audible snore escaping her well-shaped mouth, which made me giggle - I knew she would be appalled. My noise stirred Victoria, and she sat up with a start.

"I wasn't snoring, was I?" she asked anxiously.

"Of course not," I said, trying to suppress another giggle.

"You never were a good fibber Darling," said Victoria, giggling herself now.

It was early evening, and the sun was making its decent

southwards to disappear below the horizon. Although always a glorious sight, the sky was particularly dazzling this evening, with vibrant orange and yellow hues splashed across the sky like it had been lacerated by some demented artist.

Victoria took over the coffee-making process and joined me on the verandah. She handed me a mug of the steaming pungent liquid, which I accepted gratefully.

"This really is a stunning part of the world," she said wistfully. "I can totally see why you came here." She was about to say something else when a car swung smoothly into the drive. It was Matt and attached to the back of his car was a small trailer. Matt exited his car with equal smoothness, and striding towards us said cheerfully,

"I've brought you a present," nodding towards the trailer.

"What is it?" I asked, half with excitement, half with irritation. Who did he think he was coming here with gifts?

"A refrigerator," he said, grinning from ear to ear. "You can have ice on tap now."

"I can't accept that," I continued, "It's too expensive, and I, I" Matt cut me short.

"It's not brand new," he said, "I had my kitchen redone, and this is my old fridge, it's not huge, but there's nothing wrong with it and it would be a waste to dump it."

"Doesn't anyone else need it," I continued abruptly, aware of Victoria's incredulous gaze. "Everyone else is all fridged up," said Matt, a hurt look starting to creep across his chiselled face.

"Don't you want it?" Adding after a slight pause, "You could call it a housewarming present."

Suddenly I felt ashamed of myself, he was only trying to help, it really was very thoughtful of him, and I couldn't deny that a fridge would make things so much easier here. I had been making do until I could afford one, and now the prospect of all the wonderful foodstuffs I could cram into it, as well as chilling wine and tonic water and having ice at the opening of a door seduced me.

"Oh, I'm so sorry," I apologised. "It's been a strange day, please forgive me, won't you come in for a drink?"

Matt's face lit up with a beam of pleasure.

"I'd love that," he retorted. "Why don't you pour me a glass of wine and maybe Victoria will help me in with this controversial item," he added playfully.

They were both at the back of the car then, manipulating the fridge out of the trailer and into my kitchen, with Matt instructing Victoria how to negotiate the door openings.

Matt had taken me rather aback, as when I had offered him a drink, I had meant coffee, but he had requested wine, and I didn't really want to share any of "Amelia's Hill" with him, or anybody else for that matter quite yet.

Would it be churlish not to give him a glass? I wondered. Then, with a flash, I remembered the bottle of Côtes du Rhône that Victoria had brought with her – he could have a glass of that.

I had stashed it in the mahogany sideboard in the dining room, which was another treasure my mum had always loved, but just as I was reaching into the polished interior Matt's voice came wonderingly from the living room.

"What's been going on here then? Looks like you've had quite a session."

Before I could stop her Victoria had blurted out all about the shed, finding the wine equipment and the wine. Thankfully, she hadn't mentioned the box, but now she was telling him about the tasting and what that had thrown up. To my surprise Matt was following all her wine jargon without hesitation, seemingly knowing entirely what she was on about.

The scenario seemed to be unfolding like a dream in front of my eyes, and I was powerless to stop it. Victoria had now poured Matt a glass of wine and he was swirling and nosing like a pro. Finally, he took a swig and breathed in air through his lips in the exact same way as Victoria did, and then swallowed. A look of astonishment ignited his face.

"Good heavens, that's an incredible drop, tastes like a Grand Cru Burgundy," he said in awe.

"That's the 2015, which was a fantastic year in Burgundy," gasped Victoria with elation. "Wait till you taste the 2005."

"Excuse me you two," I butted in tersely, "but this is all a recent discovery, like a secret really, and I had wanted to keep it that way for the time being."

Victoria looked crest-fallen; she knew she had overstepped the mark.

"Oh, I'm so sorry, I just got carried away, and my passion ran away with me, but"

Matt butted in then.

"It's my fault Jenny, please don't blame Victoria, I shouldn't have invited myself in like this."

"You knew about it?" I asked distrustfully.

"Oh yes, Horace's wine wasn't a secret, but his wine-making methods were," said Matt with such honesty that my iciness melted.

"But I do have something else to share with you though," he continued, looking earnest now.

"I asked Uncle Walter about what you told me. Sit down Jenny and I'll tell you."

I poured myself a glass of wine from one of the bottles on the coffee table, not knowing, or caring what vintage it was, but acutely aware of the box openly basking on the table in the rays of the extraordinary sunset streaming through the window.

15

"Before you do that Matt, let Victoria show you into the shed," I said quickly.

They both looked at me askance.

"Go on, go," I insisted. "I am sure you will be fascinated Matt. I will clear up here and then when you come back you can tell me what Walter said. I can't bear sitting in a mess." This was not true, and I could see Victoria looking at me as if there was the word "liar" tattooed on my head.

As they strolled off taking their glasses with them, I grabbed the box, went to the under-stairs cupboard and almost threw it in. I was in such a hurry to hide it that I just thrust it under the paint clothes lying on the floor.

Back in the sitting room I cleared the debris from the table wondering what Matt had to tell me. I placed the part empty glasses on the work surface by the new fridge. It only just fitted in the kitchen and stuck out proud into the room which was a bit annoying. This space had not been built with a fridge in mind. That was one of the reasons I had not bought one as I hate cluttered kitchens that "don't work." I had been waiting until I had fully decided how I would refit it.

Any way it was here now, and I was sure I would soon get used to it sticking out in front of the pantry.

Victoria and Matt were gone for a long while. I had expected them back in five minutes, but they had clearly got delayed, probably drowning in each other's knowledge of the intricacies of fine wine making. I hoped Victoria was not giving away all our hopes and plans.

After half an hour I decided that I should go and find them. As I walked towards the shed, I could see them sitting on the step engrossed in conversation. They didn't see me approaching and I heard Matt saying, "Well I wondered why she was so jumpy and nervous."

Victoria saw me first and started to get up, quickly changing the subject and falling over her words like a winter's deluge of rain.

"Well yes," she said, "You can see Jenny and I have a lot of work to do before we can really make a start."

She grabbed Matt's arm turning him towards me. He was clearly uncomfortable, with that little boy caught out look.

"Oh, I didn't hear you coming," he said.

"No, I realise that," I retorted with an icy look on my face. "What have you two been up to all this time? I thought you were coming back sooner to tell me your important news."

Again, that childlike petulance had crept into my voice.

"Yes, yes," Matt said, and a bit shamefacedly they followed me back to the house.

There was a chill in the air now and the stars were beginning their slow dance to full luminescence as we made it into the sitting room. I shut all the windows and door to stop the sandflies, moths and mosquitoes ravaging us.

I plumped down heavy hearted on the sofa letting Matt and Victoria take the harder more upright chairs.

"Well," I said, "what is this news you want to tell?"

"It's a long one," said Matt, "are you sure you want me to stay to tell you now?"

"Yes," I snapped back, "please proceed."

Over the course of the next hour Matt told us what he had discovered. He had spoken to Walter and probed the subject. He had asked Walter what his plans were now that he had not been successful in the purchase of the property that I had bought. Walter told him that he didn't want to buy any other land; he had only been interested in the purchase of what was now my homestead. Matt told him that he was surprised and asked what the draw to this land was specifically. Walter had looked shifty and indignant and had fidgeted in his chair until Matt pressed him for an answer. Walter hadn't bought property before having inherited his land from his father, so hadn't been familiar with how property purchase went. He wasn't anticipating anyone else to be interested as the land was so run down, so had put in an offer and waited to hear when the sale would go through. The real estate agent had been slack and had not got back to him when the full asking price had been offered by me. So, the first news Walter had of the sale was when the sold sign went up. He was furious both with the agent and with me. Matt still didn't know why the purchase of the land had been so important to him, it would have been a lot of extra work and he clearly didn't need the income. Whichever way Matt questioned he could get no more out of Walter, but just as it looked like he was going to say something else, Clare came into the room to offer them tea and the conversation ended. Walter was clearly uncomfortable and was not going to discuss the matter further in front of her.

After Matt had finished retelling this, I asked him,
"What do you think he is hiding, and do you think he has it in for me?"
Matt shrugged and looked perplexed.
"I don't know what he is hiding; it seemed as if it was something personal. I didn't get a chance to quiz him about your suspicion that he is watching you and I didn't tell him about the rat, I was about to when Clare came in and then I had lost the opportunity."
We were all tired now, the sort of tired you get when you have drunk too much wine at lunch time and not eaten since. I decided I would just go to bed. I had experienced enough emotions for one day and I could not think straight. There were so many more questions to ask but they would have to wait until my brain was not in overload. They would wait. I took a sleeping pill I found in the bottom of my medical kit and climbed up the stairs leaving Victoria and Matt finishing off a bottle of wine.

16

As I opened my eyes to the new day, I felt dreamily relaxed. I had had a sound night's sleep and been enjoying a languid dream about walking through woods and meadows back in the sleepy Sussex village where I grew up. At first the sunlight filtering through the pastel patterned curtains that had hung in my bedroom in that childhood home tricked me into thinking I was still there. But now, as my brain realised I was awake, the memory of what had gone on the night before shattered my musing and I sat up with a gasp.
I got up and dressed hastily in jeans and a sky blue t-shirt that

enhanced the colour of my azure eyes.

I found Victoria sitting out on the Verandah drinking coffee and having heard my approach she poured a cup and offered it to me with apprehensive eyes.

"Peace offering," she said softly.

I reached out and took the cup in both hands. Finding the warm surface comforting and my mood began to thaw.

I could never be cross with Victoria for long. I knew that she would always be there for me, and trusted her implicitly, but I remained irritated as I thought she was keeping something from me.

"So what were you talking to Matt for so long about last night then?" I said, trying to keep the terseness out of my voice. "You looked like you were enjoying yourselves."

"I didn't tell him anything about the plans for the vermouth, or finding the box," she said solidly. "Matt was perplexed at your behavior, so I just mentioned about the tapping noise frightening you as an explanation for your inhospitality, and sensing his guard was down, I thought I would casually try to wheedle any information I could out of him."

I softened completely now, how on earth could I ever doubt Victoria. I knew she always had my back, and when she was in full flow, could be very persuasive indeed. I knew that innocent look from her large eyes and the way her ebullient conversation could lead people to disclose much more than they really wanted to.

"He's also troubled by what his uncle told him," Victoria continued, "or rather what he didn't tell him. If Auntie Clare hadn't come in when she did, Matt is convinced that Walter was going to tell him something really important."

Victoria relayed that Matt had caught a brief, but precise look

Clare had given Walter. It seemed like a warning look, with a glint of pure steel, and it was a look that he had never seen in his aunt's eyes before. This had unsettled him as Clare had always been his idea of a sweet old lady who spent her time almost smothering her family, looking after them baking and sewing and wouldn't hurt a fly. Matt had seen another side to her then and it weighed on his mind uneasily. Victoria said that she had stayed up drinking with Matt in the hope of finding out some more details, anything that might shed some light on the situation that was disturbingly unfolding.

"Well, did you find out anything?" I said hopefully.

"Only that Walter and Amelia were once engaged, but Amelia broke it off when she heard that Walter had been seeing Clare behind his back. Walter always denied this, but doubt and mistrust had clouded Amelia's judgement."

Victoria went on to say that Matt had been told this just recently by his father Martin, who of course was Walter's brother. Following the rat incident Matt had told his father about what you had said about Walter and asked if he could clarify any of it. Apparently, Walter had persistently tried to get back with Amelia, but she had turned to her childhood friend Horace for support. He had always held a torch for her, and within a year they were married.

Walter was beside himself with grief and jealously, and went completely off the rails, turning to drink and street brawls with anyone who looked at him sideways. Clare was always there to comfort him though, so eventually they married too – but this was almost three years later. Walter had been reluctant to commit to Clare, but she had worn him down like a stealthy predator. Martin had never liked Clare and advised against the marriage, but

Walter had seen no way out, and went ahead anyway when Clare became pregnant with Simon. Clare loathed being neighbours with Horace and Amelia, and had always badgered Walter to buy their homestead, but Horace would never sell.

There were times early on when Walter and Horace nearly made up, apparently Amelia was keen to let bygones be bygones, but Clare always put a spanner in the works somehow. Matt planned to question his father more about the matter when he next visited; he felt there was much more to the story.

Musing over what Victoria had told me we made breakfast together – the fridge jutting out accusingly like the "elephant in the room." Mentioning this idiom to Victoria made us both laugh. Ten minutes later we sat down to poached eggs on thickly buttered toast. I bought my eggs from Mason's, the same farm as I sourced my butter and other diary produce. The rich canary yellow of the yolks a stark contrast to the dazzling whites of the fresh free-range eggs.

Victoria made more coffee, I always marveled at how strong she liked to drink it.

"Well," she said, raising a quizzical eyebrow, "there is another elephant in the room, but I don't know where it's gone."

I knew exactly what she meant and went at once to the under stairs cupboard. For a moment a fear crept up my spine that it may not be there, but there it was, resting ungainly under the paint clothes where I had hastily thrown it the night before. Gathering up the box, I took my prize into Victoria, setting it down gently once more on the coffee table. We both examined it with more attention now. The carving in the shape of what looked like intricate unravelling spirals was ethereal. The tiny fragments of lustrous pāua shell shone mesmerisingly green and blue in the sunlight shining in through the open window. It was breathtakingly beautiful.

"I wonder what's in it," Victoria said whimsically.

"We have to open it first," I responded, the strident tone of my voice made Victoria jump, spilling some of her black coffee down the front of her green top.

"I've a feeling the key is hidden around here somewhere, just like the box was hidden, and we are going to find it!"

17.

This was going to be a difficult hunt. I thought it unlikely that it was in the house because I had cleaned it from top to bottom when I had moved in. Taking up the old carpets where they existed and ripping out the grimy lino from the kitchen and back porch area. As much as l liked the old house for its idiosyncrasies, I wanted it to be clean and fresh and feel as if it belonged to me.

I said to Victoria,

"Let's give it today to look for it and if we can't find it then we will have to break into it."

I hoped that we would find the key as somehow, I had come to think of the box as sacred in some way. I hadn't been in New Zealand all my life, but I had never seen anything like this box. However through my readings I was familiar with Maori culture and artefacts. The box felt as if it symbolised something important.

"Victoria, let's start looking in the shed," I suggested. "It is the place that I haven't looked at closely." Even as I was saying it, I thought why would you put a key near the place you had hidden something, but Victoria was happy to start there if I dealt with the cobwebs.

I retrieved my cleaning material from the outhouse, and we trundled down the stone pathway to the shed. The sun, still low in the sky was attempting to prise itself through some lingering clouds. It felt hopeful that the day would be fine and warm again. I was mindful that at this part of April the autumn would quickly be upon us.

 As I cranked open the door, I heard Victoria exclaim behind me,

"Oh my, look at this, it's amazing!"

I turned and saw a large Monarch butterfly on her arm. From where I was stood it looked as if it was trying to climb her arm. It then opened its wings and fluttered onto the brightly coloured Alice band on her head.

"Stand still," I ordered quietly, "I am sure it must be good luck to have a butterfly land on you." She stood stock still until it opened its wings again and flew in through the open door of the shed.

"What a fantastic start to the day," she breathed.

"Yes, indeed it does feel as if it is a good portend," I said.

"Let's go in and get on with the job of finding this key."

I moved ahead of Victoria removing cobwebs and giving cursory glances in crevices, under tables and on top of windows while Victoria undertook a more in-depth search behind me. Victoria had always been good at the detail whilst I was a broad stroke person a "let us give it a go" type. But I quickly became bored with the detail.

As we moved through the space I tried to think where Horace would have hidden the key. It then struck me that I was assuming; it might not have been Horace. It could have been Amelia or anyone else who had access to the building. As I moved to the far corner above the hole in the ground where we had found the box I saw the butterfly, it was resting on the top beams, its wings opening and shutting like a slow motion fairy learning to fly.

I stopped, mesmerised by the slow gentle movement.

"Hey Victoria," I said, "Have you ever heard of butterflies being spiritual entities?"

"No," she said, "You know me Jenny; I avoid all that mumbo jumbo rigmarole. I don't have any truck with anything spiritual."

"You wouldn't do well here in New Zealand then, there are extraordinarily strong spiritual beliefs in the Maori traditions."

"I don't know," she said, "it is mostly organised religious belief that I struggle with. I sense that indigenous peoples all over the world are more highly attuned to the natural world and develop beliefs that help them make sense of what is important in nature to them."

"Do you know when I first arrived here in New Zealand, I was petrified that I would feel homesick and have to turn around after a year and go back with my tail between my legs. But as I stepped off the plane, I felt rooted to the soil, the ground, the whenua."

"It's certainly a place that holds you in awe of nature's marvels," she agreed.

Whilst we had been talking the butterfly fluttered to my feet on the edge of the hole and then wafted on the wind towards and out of the shed door. It seemed like an appropriate time to take a break and go inside for some lunch, so we followed it and watched as it landed on an upright wooden stake that was supporting the vines.

We ate the remains of the local cheese, made across the valley from the homestead and newly marketed by the creamery. Boutique cheese was unusual in NZ and it was one of the few things I missed from the UK, good reasonably priced local cheeses. The bread was a bit stale. I needed to get my act together with the shopping. I had lost my usual sense of preparedness since Victoria had been here; we had been so engrossed in our thoughts of wine production.

"Do you think we should keep on searching for the key to this box, it could be anywhere?" Victoria asked me.

"I was thinking whist we were cleaning that it could be anywhere or nowhere; it could have been lost or thrown away," I said. "Let's try and get into the box without damaging it too much."

We had been so engrossed in eating and thinking that we hadn't heard Matt pull up. There was a rap on the door quickly followed by a now familiar voce calling out,

"Hi, can I come in? I was just on my way back to Auckland and I wanted to see if you were both OK."

Before we could move, he was in the room peering at us. This time he couldn't miss the box, it was clearly sat on the table in front of us and we had both been staring at it.

"Wow, that's a good example of a wakahuia box," he said. "You don't see many with that quality of detail on it, the carving is very unusual."

"Is it yours?" he asked looking directly at me

"No, well yes, no what did you call it?" I spluttered.

"A wakahuia box, it is a Maori treasure or feather box. The

name comes from the word waka meaning container or vessel and huia bird, which as you know is now extinct. The boxes were traditionally carved to hold feathers from the headdresses of prominent people and tonga gifts. They were usually hung from rafters for safe keeping."

"Well," Victoria blurted "We found this one in a hole in the ground in the shed. It looked as if it hand been deliberately buried."

I looked at her aghast, she looked red faced and flushed with excitement.

"What has it got in it?" Matt said.

"We don't know because we can't open it," I said, having decided that it was no good trying to hide this from him now.

"Oh it's easy," he said, "You just press these two pins at either end like this and the pretend locks spring open and," with that the box gently opened. We could all see now what it contained; the preserved remains of three butterflies.

18.

As all three of us craned our necks forward to peer inside. I was conscious of the side of my head brushing against Matt's cheek, but neither of us made any attempt to adjust our position. The chatoyant wings of the delicate creatures inside the box mesmerised us all into stillness and silence.

Victoria was the first to break the spell.

"They're absolutely enchanting!" she gasped dreamily, then on a more pragmatic note, "Anyone know anything about butterflies?"

Matt sat down on the sofa and Victoria and I automatically plonked down either side of him. He was still holding the box in both hands.

"Growing up with access to my uncle's farm enabled me to have a contact with nature that city kids don't experience," he said wistfully, as if childhood memories were filling his mind with images that only he could see.

"Uncle Walter is a great lepidopterist, and he taught me a lot about our native and endemic butterflies."

"That one," Victoria said, pointing a finger at orange-brown wings, broken by bands of black and white spots, its lower wings marked with small blue eye-spots ringed with black, "looks quite familiar."

"Yes," said Matt. "That's an Australian Painted Lady, similar to the Painted Lady butterflies that are casual visitors to Britain in your spring, its native here."

"This one," he continued, pointing to a small violet-blue specimen, "is a young male Southern Blue, the males have stronger blue colouring than the females, and they lose their colour with age. It's New Zealand's only endemic blue butterfly and is rare now."

The last butterfly in the box looked quite insignificant against the resplendent colours of its companions, with its luminous white wings marked with a distribution of small black dots.

"That's a female Small White," Matt carried on, "They were introduced here, they're what you call Cabbage Whites, and they can be a pest for cabbage farmers."

The three of us continued looking at the butterflies speculatively, each locked in our own thoughts.

"I don't know much about Maori culture," I broke in, "I know that butterflies are symbolic to the Native American peoples, but I didn't think they were hugely significant to the Maori."

"Well," Matt answered, "that is true, but did you know that they are also symbolic in Celtic culture?"

Victoria and I gazed at Matt, transfixed by what he was saying.

"For the Celts butterflies represented prosperity, good fortune, joy and honour, and symbolised the soul. In Ireland up to the 17th century it was against common law to kill a white butterfly, as they were believed to hold the souls of dead children, and it was considered bad luck to harm one. Irish folklore also says that butterflies can pass easily between this world and the next, and they are the souls of the dead returning to visit their favourite places."

"Have you got Celtic routes then?" Victoria asked quizzically.

"No, I haven't, but Amelia did, and Clare has too. It was my aunt who told me about Irish folklore – I was completely fascinated by her stories as a kid."

Victoria was looking up at Matt with glazed eyes, but then her signature practical trait surfaced.

"Coffee," she said emphatically. "We need coffee", and with that she disappeared into the kitchen.

I turned to Matt, whose hazel eyes were surveying me with a compelling look.

"What?" I asked hesitantly.

"It's your eyes," he said wonderingly, "in this light they are the colour of that Southern Blue."

19

I quickly averted my gaze. I could feel the heat rising up my neck. Soon my face would suffuse with red and I didn't want Matt to see me embarrassed.

"Well yours look like poo," I said, and as I said it I could feel a giggle coming on. I had never been any good at accepting compliments and certainly not from someone who was sat so close to me. I really wasn't looking for another romantic entanglement. I was happy on my own, or so I kept telling myself.

Matt looked hurt and stood up abruptly. Victoria returned with the coffee and immediately sensed something was wrong.

"Hey what has just gone on here? I leave you for a few minutes and when I come back the room is no longer full of sunshine and hope but icicles."

"Sorry," I said. "My fault, I think. My sense of humour doesn't always find the right place to express itself."

"Sit down Matt," I asked, "and please have a coffee with us before you leave."

Matt slumped down still looking crestfallen.

I sat looking into the room wondering how on earth I had come to this place where I was rude to people who were trying to be nice to me.

I had known Victoria for such a long time, and she tolerated my foibles. We had been good friends both at work and socially for twenty years before I came to New Zealand.

She had been married to Augustus for thirty-five years. He was tall dark and particularly good humoured. He was her perfect match and he adored her. Her world had been torn apart last year when he announced that he was going to fulfil his lifetime's ambition to sail around the world. Initially Victoria was furious and contested that he had never told her that he wanted to sail around the world, and he was being selfish. But it didn't matter what she said or how she berated him, he was determined. So, he had set off last spring in a 60-foot catamaran on his own to conquer the sea. Victoria had never been good at sea, getting very seasick; in fact, she had told me once that she felt sick if she walked on a pier. When she first told me about his plans, she was so angry and told me it would have been better if he had gone off with another woman, at least she would have stood a chance of winning him back. But to have lost him to the sea was ridiculous and demeaning.

She was shocked that he had bought a boat and done all the planning without talking to her about it at all. Where had he got the money from, she asked him, why so secretive? He told her that he had won the money on Lotto, and hadn't told her knowing that she would not have wanted to join him and would have tried to scupper his plans. She felt totally cheated and humiliated. After the initial anger and hurt Victoria who was very self-assured in her own worth as a person and was very resilient, soon concluded that she would just do her own thing and sod him, she might not be there when he returned in a years' time.

In the vacuum left by Augustus' sea going adventure we had agreed that she would come and help me for six months. I would tap into her skill and expertise in the wine making business; if she couldn't help me make it work no one could.

I knew so much about her, but what did I know about Matt? Nothing!

Sitting in the sun in my front room I resolved there and then that before I did much more, I would find out more about him and perhaps of the other inhabitants of this small settlement.

20.

"Has anyone seen Isis?" said Victoria, casually looking around the room.

"She was about yesterday," I answered. "She sometimes goes off for a wander though."

Isis was a great hunter, and sometimes just disappeared for a couple of days, returning with some "present" for me – she'd even been known to catch a rat or two before now.

I had never been worried about her before, but now a feeling of utter foreboding came over me, and I rushed out onto the verandah calling her name at the top of my voice. Nothing!

Hastily returning to the kitchen, I retrieved the box of her cat biscuits and ran out onto the verandah again, shaking them furiously – she usually never failed to come running at that tantalizing sound, and the promise of her favourite treat. Still nothing!

Starting to feel hysterical now I turned to Matt and Victoria, who had both followed me outside and were casting anxious eyes around the property and calling my precious cat's name in strained voices.

Just then I glimpsed something fluttering in the wind almost out of sight on the far side of the shed, nearly, but not quite hidden from view by the shadow the old building was casting.

Instantly I knew what it was, and we all ran down the stone pathway, my fear seeming to propel me with a speed I didn't know I was capable of. I was the first to reach her.

Lying stretched out on the grass her pink tongue protruding from her mouth, starkly contrasted against the ebony of her thick fur, was my cherished cat. There was a frothy substance emanating from her mouth, and pinned to her red collar was a note, written on the same buff paper as before, in what looked like the same handwriting.

This time it said, "Leave Bitch" in bold letters. I knew immediately that Isis was dead and now began to make high-pitched mewing noises, and then, tilting my head fully backwards looking up to the cloudless sky, a primeval scream erupted from my dry throat, shattering the idyllic landscape.

"Take Jenny inside," Matt said urgently to Victoria. "I'll deal with this."

Victoria threw an arm around me, and bundled me back into the house, then sat holding me on the sofa whist I cried, and cried, trying to talk between sobs, but not managing to say anything that made any sense.

"Shush, there, there," said Victoria, rubbing and patting my back like a mother trying to sooth her baby.

Matt came in then.

"Is there any brandy anywhere Victoria," he said quietly. Victoria dutifully went and fetched a bottle of Three Barrels from the cupboard I kept my spirits in and poured a generous measure into one of the cut glass brandy balloons that had been part of my mother's enviable glass collection.

Taking the glass from her Matt approached me gently.

"Drink this," he said softly. Without protestation I accepted and downed the strong amber liquid in one gulp, and on draining the last bit of alcohol, coughed harshly.

"What, what did they do to her?" I stammered, "She must have been in such pain."

"I don't think she would have suffered too much," Matt said. "She's been poisoned, but I think they used aconite. With large doses death is almost instantaneous. I believe someone's made a tincture from the plant and injected it into some cat food – I could still see remnants of the food in her mouth."

"How do you know all this?" I demanded sharply.

"I'm a vet," Matt said simply.

21

I started to blubber again. The thought of someone deliberately poisoning Isis was almost too much to bear.

I became suspicious of Matt thinking that if he was a vet and knew about all these kinds of things perhaps, he had poisoned her. It was odd that on both the occasions that we had found the mutilated animals he had been in the vicinity, perhaps there was some reason he wanted me out of here.

I loved that cat with a love that was deeper than any emotions that I had had for any human, and now she was gone, unutterably absolutely gone. My body heaved with deep dry sobs. Victoria was sitting still by my side, gently rubbing my back. She knew that this would be the hardest thing that I had ever endured.

She said to Matt, "I think it best if you go now, you should make your way back up to Auckland. When are you expecting to return?"

"Next weekend," he said. "It's Sarah's 30th birthday and we are having a party to celebrate."

Victoria left my side and showed Matt to the door, I heard her talking in a muffled voice, but I couldn't catch what she was saying. She entered the room looking very pale and nervous; despite my own distress I could see that she was shaken and upset.

"What did you say to him? I asked.

"Oh, nothing much," she muttered.

"Yes, you did," I said, "I heard you."

She did not want to answer me but seeing how my distress was growing again she said,

"I asked him if he could think of anyone who might have done this and he shook his head, but said whoever it was had a good knowledge of poisons and that we should be very warry for our own safety."

This set me off again crying and screaming.

"This is worse than all those miscarriages I had," I said. "At least with those I felt it was fate and that I wasn't destined to have children. Isis was my soul mate the single entity that had never pestered me and had been with me through all the challenging times."

All Victoria could do is look on. Eventually she said,

"Look its mid-afternoon now, we need to try and make sense of all of this as best we can. I think we should get some air, it might help us to process what has happened."

She took my arm and led me outside away from where Isis had been found. We walked towards the shed looking down across the valley. I could hardly see out of my swollen eyes, but the fresh air was seeping into me and reinvigorating my senses.

I told Victoria my fears about Matt.

"Do you think I'm going mad again?" I asked. "I don't seem to be able to trust anyone or myself now. You know how I was after I divorced Frank; I lost myself and any reality that might have gone with it. I was 'elsewhere' for many months."

"Yes, darling I know," Victoria said, "but you mustn't think that that will return again. You spent those few weeks in hospital and after you came and stayed with me, you found yourself again in a few months. This isn't going to be like that. You are much stronger now."

I thought about the butterfly landing on Victoria yesterday and said to her,

"You know butterflies landing on you are a sign of good luck, well you always have the good luck."

"I don't think Augustus leaving me was good luck," she said, "and both my grown-up children are living abroad. That is not lucky. I have had my share of not so good things happen. It's how we move on from the traumatic events, the stories we tell ourselves about having luck or not having it that can alter our perception of how we are in the world. You need to find a way to tell yourself a different story, not the one that goes 'I am going mad again' darling."

"Yes, I know that you are right. But it has been shitty hasn't it?"

"Yes, it has, did you want to give Isis a proper burial today, or would you rather wait until later in the week?"

"No, I think we should do it now. If I dig the hole will you go and get her and wrap her in old newspaper; there is some under the stairs. That way I don't have to see her."

Victoria rushed off towards the house whilst I got a spade out of the shed. I thought I would bury her somewhere that overlooked the view down into the valley. I needed to dig the hole deep enough so that she didn't get dug up by rats or possums. I knew that the soil over by the start of the vines was less compacted than other areas in the garden, so I wandered over to the first post where the butterfly had landed yesterday and started digging.

I had dug down about a spades depth when I hit something hard. My next spadesful of soil contained white and grey bits which I picked out of the soil with my hands, finding a thin tiny bone about the length of my little finger, and another couple of pieces that fell off it as I struggled to separate them from the soil. I sat back on my haunches in the now dampening grass as Victoria joined me.

"I am going to have to dig another hole," I said. "This one already contains bones; someone has buried another animal here at some point."

Victoria looked down at the bone fragments in my hand and said, "What kind of animal would have bones like that?"

At the same moment our eyes met, and we both knew that these were not animal remains.

22.

"They are human remains Jenny," Victoria said in a muted, barely audible voice.

"I would say they are the remains of a baby, if not a year old, then just over that." She had studied anatomy as part of her occupational therapy training.

As I nodded in stunned agreement an icy shiver passed through my body, and not knowing quite what to do, I glanced up at Victoria with imploring eyes.

"Let's put these back for now," said the practical Victoria. "We need to think carefully about what we do, and who we tell about this."

So that is what we did. Carefully replacing the tiny, brittle bones exactly where they had lain, and reinstating the earth over them, we returned them to their resting place, where they had slumbered for how many years?

Then Victoria buried Isis, in a spot I indicated just down the hill. It was a place where she used to enjoy the sun, stretching out contentedly; her black fur taking on a burnished glow in the light. I stood over her grave and muttered some silent words to the cold ground. My beautiful, Isis, named after the goddess of wisdom, she had been my faithful companion through all the good times and the bad. Now she was gone, leaving a gaping empty chasm that I didn't think could ever be filled again.

Over the next few days, we busied ourselves with the jobs that needed doing around the property. I painted walls, varnished woodwork, and ran up curtains, and Victoria prepared to harvest the vines from Amelia's Hill. Being in the southern hemisphere grapes needed to be picked in the autumn here, and an advertisement put up in the window of the store had yielded half a dozen energetic local youths to help Victoria pick the grapes. She had meticulously cleaned all the equipment in the shed, it was all still in good working order she said, and we agreed that she would make two batches of wine; one as a red pinot noir to drink as a still table wine, and one by lightly pressing the grapes to make a white wine to experiment with for our vermouth.

Victoria had explained to me that although the skins of pinot noir grapes, and indeed the vast majority of black grapes are dark, the flesh inside is white, and you could therefore make a white wine from red grapes, if you press gently and have no skin contact - like they do with champagne. Victoria knew what she was doing, and I was grateful to let her get on with it and give my bereft life a focus.

It was Thursday evening, when we had finished our chores for the day, and were sitting on the verandah watching another spectacular sunset with G&T's in hand, each lost in our own thoughts, when Matt's car swung into the drive.

He got out and approached us tentatively.

"How are you Jenny?" he said sincerely, giving Victoria a nod as he came up the steps.

"Getting on with life," I said, trying to sound resolute. "What brings you here this evening?"

Glancing at Victoria he asked,

"Can I have one of those?" gesturing at the drink in her hand.

"Of course," she responded, not waiting to see if that was OK with me and skipped off inside. Matt sat down beside me on one of the old wicker chairs that adorned the verandah.

"I'm not sure if this is appropriate or not now," he said carefully, "but I asked Sarah if I could bring a couple of guests with me to her party. I thought it might be an good time for you and Victoria to meet some of your neighbours, including the Pharaoh clan, but I'll understand if you don't want to."

The gin had made my mind feel sluggish, but it cleared now with a sudden burst of clarity. This would be the perfect opportunity to do exactly what Matt was proposing – Victoria and I would be able to meet Walter and Clare in a perfectly normal situation, and we would both be able to confer together afterwards about whatever transpired.

"No, we would love to," I told Matt in a voice that sounded much stronger than I felt.

"Oh great," he said brightly, the worried look he had worn since he arrived dispersing.

"I'll let Sarah know, but there is something else I would like to share with you."

"Oh," I inquired, raising a quizzical eyebrow.

"Can I pop by tomorrow morning; I'm tired now, after the long drive."

"If you like, would after breakfast, say 9.30 be OK with you?" I said lightly.

"Perfect," he replied, and with that I watched him return to his car and drive off in the crepuscular light towards the Pharaoh homestead. Just then Victoria returned with Matt's drink.

"What, where's he gone?" she began, but I broke in hastily, "Never mind about that," exchanging the fresh glass of G&T she held in her hand with the empty one I had just drained.

I was waiting for Matt on the verandah when he returned the following morning on the dot of 9.30, dressed in sky blue shorts and a lilac t-shirt; the long summer had kissed my skin with a honeyed tan.

After Matt had left last night, I had told Victoria what he had said, and we had agreed that we would try and find out everything we could now about our mysterious neighbours, but we would not mention the tiny bones buried beneath the vines in their simple grave.

Now, having breakfasted with Victoria on fresh fruit and Mason's Greek style yogurt, I felt fresh and energetic - ready for what the day would bring.

"Well," I greeted him brightly, "what have you got to say that you were too tired to tell me last night?"

"Let's take a walk," he said, I thought rather pensively.

"Just over the fence there, where your land boundaries Walter's, there is a lovely walk through the meadows down to his wood."

"Won't he mind me trespassing on his land?" I asked feeling a bit alarmed.

"You're with me," Matt answered decisively, and with that we were walking down to, and over the fence, leaving the familiar territory of my land into what was for me, the uncharted territory of Walter's.

Without preamble Matt announced,

"I went to see my dad whist I was up in Auckland; I had been thinking about how the lives of Horace and Amelia, and Walter and Clare were intertwined, and I wanted to talk him about that."

Just then we came to a fork in the path. Matt was about to turn left towards the wood, but the right hand track looked more appealing to me, as you couldn't see round the corner, and wildflowers danced alluringly in the slight breeze, seeming to beckon to who knew where...

"I've never been down there," Matt said apprehensively.

"You sound a little nervous," I teased, "don't you want to know where it goes? I can't believe you haven't explored all the land round here whilst you were growing up."

"Yes, you are right, but when I was a kid Auntie Clare always said there were banshees down there," he motioned towards the track. "I guess the place always seemed malevolent to me."

Seeing my amused look Matt flushed a little and then quickly recovered and taking my arm we started to make our way down the right-hand pathway.

"Oh, it's so beautiful," I gasped as we rounded the corner and the entire vista of the valley came into view.

"It's," but Matt stopped abruptly, pulling me back behind him.

"What?" I inquired, following his gaze to a patch of beautiful hooded purple-blue flowers.

"Aconite," he said rigidly.

23.

"Well it's very pretty," I said, refusing to be thrown by the sight of all this aconite. "Is it native to New Zealand?"

"No, I don't think so. It's more widely found now but it was originally from the mountainous areas of the northern hemisphere. I don't know much about it only that it is very poisonous to animals and humans if ingested. I believe it's one of England's most deadly plants."

Matt continued quickly,

"I don't think we should linger here too long. If Auntie Clare was always scaring me off coming down here, I am guessing that she knows it's here. I don't really want to retrace our steps in case we are seen from their house. I hope if we cut back across and up through the bush here that we will come out on the other path, out of sight from their house."

Matt led the way pushing through into the bush. Initially it was easy to walk through but gradually the undergrowth got thicker with brambles and gorse cutting at our legs. I tried not to yelp too much but it was challenging work keeping a forward momentum. Matt was standing on the larger brambles to hold them down to allow me to follow behind him but it wasn't long before my lilac tee shirt was ripped and stained with crimson bloody streaks, and my bare legs were riven with bramble scratches, the blood gradually dribbling in slow streams into my socks. To make it worse we were heading uphill so I was hot, sweaty, and bloody. After a brief time, the nature of the undergrowth changed. We were now walking under tall pines with intermittent stands of long Pampas-like grass, called Toetoe.

Although it was easier going the grass wrapped itself around my legs causing me to tip forward. A couple of times Matt only just caught me as I was about to faceplant the slope. After what seemed like an interminable time, we could see the edge of the plantation and then we were out blinking in the sunlight.

Matt turned to me.

"Are you OK?"

"Do I look OK?" I retorted, "I'm hot, pestered and covered in scratches."

I started to giggle, the relief of our escape hitting me. Matt laughed too.

"Not quite what I had intended," he said. "At least now we can walk back to your house without being seen by Walter or Clare."

"I hope they can't see us," I said, "They will take one look at me and think that you have been rolling me through the brambles."

We both laughed and walked purposefully back to the house. Victoria greeted us at the door.

"Nice walk?" she started, and then seeing me gasped, "What has happened to you?"

"We will explain in a minute," we both said in unison. "Let us get in and clean ourselves up."

"Matt took me on a short cut," I said still laughing.

After I had showered and changed into a clean, but old tee-shirt and shorts, I returned downstairs.

"You don't look much better," said Victoria. "Where on earth did you get those clothes from?"

"They are my old gardening clothes," I said, "I didn't want

to get blood on any of my better clothes."

Matt had also changed into clean clothes from his car.

"I don't want to arrive at Uncle Walters looking like the wreck of the Hesperus," he said. "That would get them thinking."

"Now explain," said Victoria. We told her what we had seen and what we had done to avoid being seen.

"Oh, my goodness," she said, "why would the aconite be growing down there and in such an abundant amount?"

"That's the question that's in the forefront of my mind," said Matt. "Do you have Wi-Fi here? I think it might be an idea to find out a bit more about it than I know before we start scaring ourselves to death."

"I don't have Wi-Fi," I said. "I haven't got it connected yet, Horace didn't have it and I was seeing how I could manage without it before I committed to another big monthly bill. We have good phone signal here and I have a good data package on my phone. Shall we look?"

I googled aconite and was amazed at the number of sites that came up. Most of them detailed the extreme danger of the plant especially to children and animals. I skipped over the history of how it was named and its Turkish origins. But I did glean that it was monk's hood, one of the other names for aconite that was reported as being responsible for bringing down the Emperor Claudius. I was also not too keen on reading about how it could be used on arrows to shoot at enemies. My imagination started to run out in increasing circles of horror about what might happen to us next.

What did capture my attention was its use in Ayurveda and

traditional Chinese medicine and homeopathy.

"Homeopathy," I said incredulously, "I had a friend in England, a nurse, who did her homeopathy training. I always thought it was a bit of mumbo jumbo. How on earth can an infinitesimal amount of something help cure what in substantial amounts it's meant to cause?"

"I don't think it's as straight forward as that," said Victoria. "They have done double blind studies in cows to minimise mastitis and believe it or not the homeopathic remedy has worked."

"One thing is for certain the cows were not influenced by their belief in its efficacy," Matt said.

"Oh," Matt went on, the colour draining out of his face, "one of the things my dad did tell me was that Auntie Clare used to dabble in homeopathic cures. He didn't know too much, just mentioned it in passing."

We all fell silent.

24

Victoria had prepared a light lunch whilst we'd been gone, and now she set plates of cured meats, a dish of steaming new potatoes garnished with mint from the herb garden, dripping with melted butter, and a big bowl of green salad before us on the table under the fig tree. Soda bread, a bowl of mixed olives, and a jug of glistening olive oil completed the feast. She had set three places.

We all sat down and greedily began to tuck in, with Victoria pouring glasses of ice-cold sauvignon blanc – the refrigerator now a welcome addition to my kitchen.

Finding the aconite though had distracted Matt from the reason for his visit, and remembering this now I turned to him, a stream of melted butter dribbling down my chin which I hastily wiped away with the back of my hand.

"You said that you went to see your father to talk about Horace and Amelia, and Walter and Clare, I got the feeling that he might have told you something profound."

Matt set down his knife, he had been buttering a slice of soda bread, from which he now took a thoughtful bite, and then set that down too, even teeth marks leaving their imprint in the pale butter.

Victoria and I watched him intently as he swallowed and cleared his throat.

"What dad said has really disturbed me," Matt began, glancing at Victoria uncertainly.

"I keep no secrets from Victoria, we are all in this together now, and I want to get to the bottom of it. All this has doubled my resolve to stay here and fulfil my dream, so if anyone thinks they can oust me out, they've got another think coming!" I said with conviction.

Matt's expression changed from uncertain to determined.

"OK then, but it doesn't make for easy listening."

Matt went on to tell us that Amelia had given birth to a baby daughter, exactly nine months after her wedding day. They had called her Ailbe, which means "white" in Gaelic.

She was beautiful, and a model baby, good natured and inquisitive, and a healthy and robust child, but when she was just over a year old, she vanished, just vanished.

Amelia and Horace were beside themselves and the whole community searched high and low for her, but she was never found. Slowly Amelia and Horace began to rebuild their lives, but although they tried, they never had another child.

"There was a rumour at the time that Ailbe had been Walter's daughter. He visited Amelia the night before her wedding to try and persuade her to come back to him. Apparently he was there all night – someone saw him leaving Amelia's parents' house in the early hours of her wedding day looking dishevelled, and Amelia watching him go from her window with tears streaming down her face, but she went ahead and married Horace the same day. And the thing is, Ailbe looked just like Walter, she had the Pharaoh ice blue eyes and cleft chin."

Victoria and I were both looking at Matt's dimpled chin now, but his hazel eyes?

Matt understood our contemplative looks,

"I take after my mum with my eye colour," he said, "but if you saw dad you would see Walter's face and colouring mirrored like two peas in a pod."

"What do they think happened to Ailbe?" said Victoria, nibbling on an olive.

"To this day no one knows, and it's still occasionally talked about by people who were there at the time. It remains a great mystery - Auntie Clare told me the banshee must have taken her."

"Well," I said ponderingly, "the plot thickens – when is Sarah's party?"

"Tomorrow evening," said Matt. "I'll pick you both up at 7pm."

25.

"Where is it taking place?" I asked.

"In the back room of the bar in the village," Matt answered.

"I have never been in there; I have avoided all the local watering holes they seem to be full of pokies and sports

66

screens."

"Pokies", exclaimed Victoria, "that somehow sounds rude."

"Not rude, just diabolical," I said. "There are lots of people here in New Zealand addicted to playing them; they are what we would call one arm bandits. It's quite common for people to pour in hundreds of dollars in a sitting. They are rigged to appeal to the 'what I might win' streak in people."

"This back room is quite nice," said Matt. "It's got a small kitchen and a raised stage area."

"Is there going to be karaoke?" I asked.

"God, I hope not. I can't bear that public show of hopeless singing," Matt said sanctimoniously. I kept quiet as I quite liked it but wasn't going to say so now.

"Oh, I meant to tell you, it's a bring a plate do."

"Bring a plate?" said Victoria.

"Yes, everyone brings a plate of food to share with the group. You usually end up with stacks of food; you just hope that not everyone brings a dessert."

"I don't know," said Victoria, "I could cope with that," and we all smiled. Victoria was known for her love of all food, but she had a passion for all things sweet.

"Perhaps Victoria can do a dessert and I will do a savoury," I said. My mind immediately switched to thinking what I had in the cupboard that I could cook without having to go out shopping.

I said to Victoria, "I have some glacé chestnuts in my store cupboard, so if we got some cream from Mason's in the morning you could make that divine chestnut pudding thing I had once at your house."

"You mean the chocolate and marron glacé tart I made for

you once."

"Yes, that's it, a crisp buttery pastry case with a rich chestnut purée, cream and chocolate filing topped off with marron glacé," I said, dribbling in anticipation.

"Well I don't have the recipe," Victoria quickly interjected.

"I am sure we can find it online," I parried.

"That's that sorted then. Who else will be there do you know?" Victoria asked Matt.

"Quite a few people, some of Sarah's relatives obviously and most of the close neighbours from the road here."

"I have met Stuart and Steven from the end house only in passing; as far as I know they are an arty couple. They seem very affable and it would be good to meet them properly in a social situation. I have also met the couple on the other side down the valley who are in the process of renovating an old barn. They have two small children, a four-year-old and a new-born. If they come, they will have to bring the children, but I do hope they can come. The four-year-old Susan has the most stunning brown eyes that you have ever seen, and long brown hair just like her mums and the baby is just the cuddliest thing on the planet. Then there is another man who lives up the road from us, in my casual meetings as we walk past each other he seems OK but I have been told that he can be inappropriate to women; reminds me a bit of Frank's brother," I laughed.

"I am sure you will have a chance to talk to many people," said Matt, "not least Walter, Sarah and Simon. Well now I had better get going."

After Matt left Victoria and I sat mulling over the remarkable occurrences of the last few days.

"It all seems a bit like one of those dreams," said Victoria, You know those dreams that when you are in them you keep thinking this is all wrong, but it just keeps developing around you."

"It all seems too contrived and too dramatic to be real," I said. "This is small town New Zealand, not Massachusetts in the 17th century. We must be careful that this doesn't turn into a mass hysteria, well you and me hysteria anyway. Mutilated rats, poisoned cats, obscene notes, a box with butterflies hidden under the floor of the shed, a field of majestic but deadly aconite, and bones of a baby," I said shuddering.

"And a tall dark affable handsome stranger," Victoria added.

"Changing the subject, how's that wine making coming on? Shall we wander down so I can see what you have been up to?"

"Yep we could, what a great idea, might take our minds off all of this oddness," said Victoria.

"Do you regret coming? "I asked anxiously

"No, don't be daft I love being here."

We wrapped our fleeces around our shoulders against the dampening late afternoon air. The walk to the shed filled us with warmth, the sun dipping behind the mountain, the soft bleat of sheep, the ear filling buzzing of the bees in the late mānuka blossom; all soothed the senses.

We entered the shed and I looked around in amazement. The changes were astounding. This time last week this had been a cobwebby dusty rundown shed, now it had been metamorphosed into a smart wine making environment, all shiny, not new but shinny. Victoria had done an amazing job of utilising what was here.

"You will have to tell me tomorrow where you are up to in the process," I said, "then we can make a list of what I need to purchase to help the completion of this first vintage."

My nose tingled with the sweet aroma that I associate with fully ripe plump sultanas or raisins. It reminded me of my mum's Christmas pudding making.

 We wandered back to the house. The moths were battering themselves against the solar lighting, parting as we stepped through them like snowflakes against a car windscreen in a winter's storm.   As we sat down to eat a quickly pulled together meal of lunch leftovers I said to Victoria,

"I do wonder what tomorrow will bring. I feel quite nervous about attending the party as I haven't attended a formal gathering since I have been here. I don't even think I have anything to wear that will be suitable."

"If that is all you have to worry about you don't know how lucky you are," she retorted.

"But I have put on so much weight I feel just like a heffalump, and nothing sits comfortably on me," I moaned.

"We will cross that bridge tomorrow. Can you squeeze another glass of this delightful pinot gris from Nelson into your torso?" Victoria tempted.

"Oh don't," I said laughing, "That's most of my weight problem - my alcohol consumption."

26.

The kitchen was filled with mingling sweet and savoury scents. Victoria had been busy making her chocolate marron glacé tart, much relieved that I had found a recipe online for her to follow. Victoria was an excellent cook, but she liked the boundaries of a recipe, which she followed rigidly, hating to substitute ingredients if she didn't have them to hand, and was hopeless at creating spontaneous dishes from her imagination. This is where I came into my own. I had always been able to conjure up "something from nothing" and the finished dishes always seemed to taste so good that the recipients often asked me for the recipe!

So, I had made a three cheese quiche, constructed from odd remnants of cheese I found strewn throughout the fridge, artistically decorated with the leftover olives from yesterday's lunch.

The rest of the day passed quickly, with Victoria attending to her wine-making tasks, and me weeding the herb garden, and putting the finishing touches to the new curtains I was making for the bedroom that Victoria now occupied.

It was now late afternoon and having both showered Victoria and I were both in our prospective bedrooms with damp skin and newly washed hair, frantically rummaging through our clothes, trying to find something suitable to wear to Sarah's party.

Victoria emerged first, resplendent in a silk dove grey cap-sleeved number embroidered with vibrant hummingbirds. She had applied forest green eyeshadow and a soft pink lipstick, which made her alluring face look radiant.

"Wow, you look beautiful," I said appreciatively. I was still standing by my open wardrobe in my underwear.

"I really haven't got a clue what to wear," I mumbled, waving my arms at the clothes hanging up in front of me.

Victoria came in and started to examine the contents of my wardrobe with expert hands.

"Put your face on Jenny," she said with authority, and I duly obeyed whilst she rustled about muttering almost imperceptibly to herself with the odd expletive escaping from her pursed lips. Finally, she brought out a purple and green floaty sleeveless dress, with a handkerchief hem, sprinkled with silver sequins that caught the light coming in through the open window.

Taking it from her, and slipping it over my head, I admired my reflection in the Edwardian cheval mirror in the corner of the room.

"I'd forgotten I had that," I marvelled, "I've always loved this dress."

The diaphanous material skimmed over my tanned body, oscillating seductively as I moved, and its colours complimented the slick of lime green eyeshadow I'd applied with my signature coral lipstick accentuating my cupids bow mouth.

"You look stunning Jenny," breathed Victoria, "absolutely stunning."

Then we both wafted down the stairs into the living room in a haze of perfume, giggling like schoolgirls going to our first gown up party. Victoria fixed G&T's "to steady our nerves" she said, still chortling. I accepted the glass from her outstretched hand gratefully and began to imbibe the cold aromatic nectar.

Just then, hearing a car on the drive, we both downed our drinks and went out onto the verandah, just in time to see Matt getting out of his car. He looked striking, dressed in beige chinos and an open necked Tyrian purple shirt.

"Oh Jenny, he's dressed to match you," Victoria giggled. Giving her a hasty dig in the ribs I shouted a confident greeting to Matt. Turning, he stopped dead in his tracks.

"What's up?" I called breezily.

"You look amazing," he said, almost in a whisper, staring straight at me.

"She scrubs up well doesn't she," said Victoria, skipping by me and down the steps trying unsuccessfully to subdue her giggles. She jumped into the back of the car and settled down next to a jumble of boxes and male paraphernalia, leaving me no option than to sit in the front next to Matt.

"Can't get the staff; give me a hand with these would you?" I nodded to Matt, indicating the dishes we had made, nestling in Tupperware boxes on the verandah table. He dutifully transferred them into his boot, and then chivalrously held the passenger door open for me.

"Your carriage awaits," he said with due ceremony, and I got in feeling rather thrilled.

The feeling didn't last though. As we drove towards the village apprehension began to encroach into my previous light mood, and by the time we pulled up in front of the bar, I felt quite sombre.

Matt held the door open again for me, leaving Victoria to fend for herself, and I alighted from his car with a heavy heart, wondering what the evening would bring. Then Victoria and I, each taking one of Matt's proffered arms, entered the bar with him grinning between us like the cat that's got the cream.

"Sarah," Matt called out happily to a rather short dumpy young woman with mousy hair on the far side of the room, who now made her way towards us. She was wearing a shapeless muted orange and yellow patterned dress that reminded me of curtains that used to hang in my grandmother's house, but round her neck shone a beautiful, rounded quadrilateral shaped pendent in gold. As Matt introduced us her already small eyes narrowed even more. Sarah glanced up at Matt.

"When you asked to bring a couple of guests, I didn't realise it was our neighbours," she said, I thought rather sarcastically, but then brightened,

"Good to meet you both," extending a clammy hand to Victoria first then me.

"I've been eager to meet you, but please excuse me for a while, I've got to sort out the catering," and with that she bustled off in the direction of the kitchen.

"Well, she looks like a bundle of laughs," I commented, just as a handsome young man with ice blue eyes came up behind Matt and slapped him on the back playfully, grinning mischievously.

"Where have you been hiding these two beauties?" he said impishly, "You dark horse," Matt flushed.

"It's ..."

"Simon," I interrupted him, "can't mistake that Pharaoh colouring."

Simon's open face was the opposite of Sarah's sharp features, and as he grasped our hands, he seemed genuinely pleased to meet us. He was about to say something else when Sarah's shrill voice called him from the kitchen.

"Better go and help out," he said ruefully. "Catch you later cuz, and you lovely ladies too," he said with a wink. "Go and get a drink – there's a free bar."

As we sipped welcome glasses of Hawke's Bay Syrah, Matt told us that Auntie Clare had all but arranged Simon's match with Sarah whose family owned hundreds of acres adjoining the Pharaoh land to the west. The Cargill's were one of the richest families in New Zealand.

Simon wasn't engaged yet though, and Clare had hoped that he

74

would propose to Sarah tonight on her 30th birthday. But Simon wasn't in love with Sarah; Matt was close to his cousin and knew that his affections rested with a lively redhead called Alana, whom he pointed out sitting at a circular table engaged in animated conversation with a group of other pretty young local girls. Suddenly a deep male voice came from over my right-hand shoulder,

"Aren't you going to introduce me to my neighbour?" it said as I tuned to meet the cold eyes of Walter Pharaoh.

"Where's Auntie Clare?" Matt said, oblivious to the chilly atmosphere Walter's arrival had created.

"She didn't feel well," Walter answered without taking those glacial eyes off me, "She thought it better if she stayed at home and rested."

"This is Jenny, and this is her friend Victoria," Matt said brightly, "Hope auntie's alright, she's missing a great party."

"Just a stomach upset, nothing serious," replied Walter. "She'll be right as rain tomorrow. By the way, she's planning a little celebration of her own tomorrow afternoon, she asked me to invite you Matt and you can bring your new acquaintances if you like, I know Clare's been keen to meet them."

As he talked Walter's demeanour seemed to soften and the cold stare began to thaw. Looking at me now he said in a quiet voice, "I know I've come over as inhospitable, hostile even, but I don't mean to be, it's just my way, I hope you understand. Please forgive a grumpy old fool. There's a bottle of Cloudy Bay's Pelorus behind the bar, please enjoy it with Victoria and Matt, and accept my apologies for making you feel awkward." Then, before I could answer, he stepped away, waving at a short corpulent man about his own age.

"That's Cyrus Cargill," said Matt, "Sarah's father. Let's crack open that Pelorus then shall we?" he continued, excitedly motioning to the young man behind the bar.

An hour later Matt and I were sitting at a table near the stage finishing off the delectable sparkling wine. He had introduced Victoria to his partner in his veterinary business. Clive was just her type, tall and dark and they hit it off immediately. I knew she was probably round the back of the building now snogging his face off. As the pulsating rhythm of Black Box's "Ride on Time" blasted out from the turntable I jumped up pulling a surprised Matt to his feet with me.

"Let's dance," I announced. I had always loved dancing, finding such joyous release in losing myself in the expression of movement.

We danced and danced; all my fears and worries of the past weeks disappearing as we rotated around each other moving in time, responding to each record that played. Matt was an expert jiver, and controlled me effortlessly, as he whirled me around the dance floor.

The tempo of the music changed then as the mesmerising notes of Procol Harum's "Whiter Shade of Pale" drifted through the air. Matt put his hands around my waist and I instinctively raised my arms to circle his neck. But just as he started to pull me nearer, a deafening scream pierced the charged atmosphere, and moments later Sarah came running into the hall with mascara running down her plump face, directly into the arms of her bewildered father. Simon entered seconds later, a vivid red mark across his left cheek.

It seemed that Victoria wasn't the only one snogging someone's face off round the back of the building. Sarah had caught Simon in the beautiful redhead's arms!

The party broke up abruptly then, with everyone making embarrassed farewells. Matt and I listened as Victoria relayed the scene that had unfolded before her and Clive as they were "talking" she said, outside.

"I suppose that puts the kybosh on Clare's get-together tomorrow then," I said in a dejected tone. I was disappointed not to have met her this evening.

"Oh no," replied Matt. "Walter told me that was still on, nosy old Mable Watkins rung auntie to gleefully tell her what happened, but that hasn't made any difference to her plans. I think it was going to be some sort of engagement celebration, but I'm not sure how that's going to go now."

"Well," said Victoria with her usual directness, "Sarah is too vanilla for Simon, she can't hold a candle to Alana, but I did like that necklace she was wearing, what was that?"

"A four-leaf clover," said Matt soberly, "A present from Auntie Clare. It's for protection."

27.

"I didn't know that clovers were meant for protection I thought that each leaf symbolised one of four things, faith, love, luck and hope," I said.

"Oh no," Matt interrupted, "in the middle ages it was thought that the bearer of a four-leaf clover could recognise witches and evil spirits and it offered protection against the evil eye."

"How do you know all this?" I asked looking at Matt sideways my old suspicions rising again.

"Sarah took great delight in telling me last Christmas when

it was given to her. Auntie Clare had had it made especially for her from a gold pendant that had been given to Clare's mother on her engagement. The gold was some of the last that came from the Karangahake mine which had some powerful significance that I didn't quite follow. She also told me that gold can enhance one's psychic abilities and that Clare thought that Sarah had these abilities."

"It didn't help her identify that Simon wasn't committed to her," I said snidely. Victoria giggled. We had both drunk too much but now that the fun of the party had been shattered, I was feeling very tired and just wanted to go home.

"Clive has invited us up to his room for a drink," Victoria said. "He is staying here in the pub for the night."

"I'm tired I would like to go home," I replied. I knew that Victoria had the staying power of a cart horse on speed when a good time and alcohol was involved; she also had the advantage over me of being able to nap or sleep anywhere, so catching up on sleep wasn't such an issue for her.

Matt said, "I can take you home Jenny. It's not far and I haven't had that much to drink, as I had planned to be your lift home."

I looked at him thoughtfully taking in his strong arms and handsome features. I was apprehensive about him taking me home alone as I wasn't sure if I would be able to resist his charms and I didn't want to fall for him or get involved. I just wasn't ready.

I wasn't making good choices or being very rational post wine and although I certainly wasn't Victoria's keeper I didn't want her making a fool of herself with Clive, she had only just met him and I had hopes for her and Augustus getting back together.

Victoria was ignoring my warning signs of irritation. She left the room hanging on Clive's arm, unusually slurring her words.

I shouted after her,

"I'll go home then and, I suppose, see you in the morning." She waved her arm at me imperiously, giggling.

"Where are you staying tonight?" I asked Matt.

"I have a room at Uncle Walters, I've stayed in it for years, it's where I always stay when I am this way."

"I have had a lovely evening," I said, "thank you for offering to take me home. It's not like Victoria to dessert me. I had thought that we would walk back together."

"She's enjoying herself too," Matt said, "and Clive is great uncomplicated company."

Really, I thought, if only life were that simple. I climbed into Matt's car beside him; we had the roof closed as the evening had turned much cooler now. It wasn't a long drive, but my mind wandered to the days when I was first with Frank. How exciting and straight forward life had seemed. I had assumed that we would have children and that we would be together forever, after all wasn't that what wedding vows were about. It's strange how life turns and takes you in different directions. Here I was now just over a year in New Zealand starting a quite different chapter in my life. Suddenly I blurted out,

"Have you ever been married Matt? You are an attractive man it seems so unusual for you to be single?"

As soon as it came out of my mouth, I regretted it. I was

making assumptions, for all I knew he had a partner; maybe I had been misreading his attentiveness.

"My work is the focus of my life now."

"Oh" I said, "I didn't mean to intrude."

"I expect I have been giving you mixed messages," he said. "You are an attractive, intelligent woman and I am very attracted to women's brains."

We had arrived at the house. Matt came around to my side of the car and opened the door. I sort of fell out, it was low to the ground and my legs didn't want to work after all that dancing. He heaved me up making sure I was steady, kissed me lightly on the cheek and said,

"I'll stay here until you are in the house and I will ring you tomorrow to let you know the details of the do that Auntie Clare is putting on."

"Thank you," I stuttered. I felt embarrassed and somewhat taken aback that he obviously didn't want to come in. I tottered to the door, found my key, waved at him and fell inside, shutting the door quickly behind me. Blast, blast and double blast I thought, I didn't want him to come in, but I wanted him to want to come in.

I made straight for my bedroom not bothering to wash or clean my teeth wondering how I managed to make a mess of relationships. I fell into bed and snuggled up to my extra-large pillow. The next thing I knew I was wide awake, very thirsty, but sure something other than my thirst had woken me.

I listened intently my ears feeling huge with the effort of listening. Nothing, I got up and cautiously went downstairs turning on the hall lights as I went. I didn't bother with the kitchen light as the moon was shining brightly in through the window and it was as clear as day. As I passed the back door, I double checked that I had locked it and it opened in my hand. I froze, I was sure I had locked it. I stood there in the open doorway looking across to the shed. Through the muted moon- dust defused light I thought I saw a pale shadowy figure standing where we had found the baby's grave. I stared hard trying to make out the shape but in the odd light it came and went in and out of focus. I felt strangely calm almost as if I had waited all my life for this moment.

A hand on my shoulder jolted me. I screamed and hit out. I heard this distant voice saying "Stop, stop it's OK." Through the mist and haze of my thick head I realised it was Victoria. "It's me," she said, "I have come back, I think you were asleep it looks as if you have been sleep -walking."

As I became focused, I realised that I was kneeling on the grass by the grave.

"Victoria we must, must do something about this poor baby we can't just ignore that we found it."

My legs were wet from the damp grass. I started to shake violently.

"Let's get inside," Victoria said, gently helping me to my feet and leading me by the arm.

28.

Once inside Victoria made strong coffee and sat me down on the sofa. I wriggled my nose as I took my first sip, tasting alcohol. She had put a nip of brandy in it.

"Good for shock," she said.

Victoria went on to say that she knew I was irritated with her for staying on with Clive, but there had been a method in the madness and she had grasped the opportunity, not to sleep with him, but to find out more about Matt.

Clive, who had turned out to be a perfect gentleman, had told Victoria that Matt had been engaged once to another vet in Auckland. She was called Louise, and not only had beauty but brains too. They made a handsome pair and seemed like a golden couple. They bought a rambling old house just outside the city and spent every weekend doing it up, taking great care to restore it to its former glory, traveling all over the country to source original fittings and furnishings. There was a beautiful round stained glass window in the middle of the house on the first floor. They had cleaned it from the inside, using cotton buds moistened in a little de-ionised water. The damp fibres collected the dirt effectively from all the intricate nooks and crannies, but the outside surface of the window remained filthy, ingrained with over a hundred years of grime and dirt. It was a delicate job, and a precarious one, the window positioned as it was above the porch. Matt said that he would do it, but he needed to get some more cotton buds first.

However, whilst Matt drove to the store, Louise must have remembered that she had some buds in her handbag, and seemingly was unable to resist making a start.

On his return Matt found her on the ground with the toppled ladder laying a few feet away from her lifeless body, along with her handbag, a cotton bud still between her fingers. The post-mortem confirmed that she had died instantly on impact with the ground.

Matt was devastated and threw himself into his work, expanding and improving the business over the last three years, making it the success it is today.

"Apparently, he's never even looked at another woman since, until…" Victoria hesitated.

"Until what?" I questioned, looking up from my coffee mug. Victoria carried on, explaining that Clive was Matt's confidante, and he had told him that he was inexplicably drawn to you. He'd tried to resist, telling himself that he wasn't ready for another relationship, but he liked your company, and had resolved to just be friends. However, Clive knew that Matt was struggling with his emotions.

I felt in conflict with my own emotions but was secretly pleased with this revelation. Victoria broke through my musings.

"You are right though Jenny, we do need to do something about the baby, do you think we should bring Matt into it?"

"Let's see what happens this afternoon," I concluded, "and thank you darling, I should have known you wouldn't have just abandoned me last night." Victoria gave me a reassuring hug before she bounded into the kitchen to make breakfast.

This time we didn't take such care in choosing what to wear, as Matt had said it would be an informal affair. When he arrived to collect us at 3.30 in the afternoon we were dressed casually, Victoria in wide legged navy linen trousers and a blue and white sailor stripped top, and me in white Capri pants and a cyan blue sleeveless blouse. Victoria, who rarely missed a trick, knew that the top accentuated the colour of my eyes, but chose not to voice her observation.

Matt suggested walking up to the Pharaoh homestead as the weather was glorious, not a cloud in the sky, with the late afternoon rays of the sun bathing us in its soft light as we made our way up the track, with the distinctive sounds of the Tui birds punctuating the still air. It was a perfect afternoon.

Matt and I were a little awkward in each other's company, trying to avoid direct eye contact as our journey progressed.

As we passed through the iron gates that flanked the entrance to the house, something caught the periphery of my vision, and I turned just in time to see a white butterfly fluttering up and over the high fence out of site. Somehow, I thought this was a good omen.

There were quite few cars parked outside the house and from the noise coming from inside, it appeared that a happy gathering was in full swing, with no suggestions of the previous night's unsettling events casting any shadows at all over the proceedings.

Just then a small slim woman with a silver bob and pale green eyes came rushing out of the front door towards us.

"Matt," she proclaimed joyfully, raising herself up on tiptoes to fling her arms round his neck and give him a tight hug.

"So glad you could make it and managed to bring our neighbours with you too."

"Auntie Clare," exclaimed Matt, easily swinging the slight frame round a couple of turns and setting it lightly back on the ground again. She wore a gold four-leaf clover pendant around her neck that was identical to the one she had gifted Sarah.

Clare was a little breathless; Matt had explained that she had a heart condition for which she took medication.

"You must be Jenny and Victoria," she continued; her face flushed with delight.

"It's the other way around," Matt laughed.

"This is Jenny, and this is Victoria."

Then on a more serious note,

"Is the engagement going ahead then Auntie? After last night I…"
"Of course it is," Clare carried on brightly, "what on earth do you mean, Simon and Sarah's union is written in the stars."
I saw Victoria's eyebrows rising out of the corner of my eye.
"Come on, let's get you some drinks," Clare purred, linking Matt's arm and pulling him through the front door. Victoria and I followed behind, a conspiratorial glance passing between us.
Clare furnished us all with a glass of Pelorus, just as a sheepish Simon came into the room. "Please excuse me won't you, I just need a word with my son." Then she marched purposefully up to Simon and bundled him into a side room off the hall, slamming the door behind them.
Victoria saw Clive across the room and went over to speak to him. Matt grabbed my arm and propelled me towards the hall.
"What are you doing?" I said a little alarmed.
"Don't you want to find out what's going on?" he whispered, bringing me to a standstill outside the door.
"Act casual," Matt continued, "as if we're just standing here chatting."
 I nodded my agreement as we both strained our ears towards the shut door. Clare's angry voice arose from within.
"Yes, you are going to marry her Simon; I'm not letting you throw your future away on a pretty face."
"I don't love Sarah mum," Simon
protested.
"This is not about love you idiot, your father never loved me, but he grew to be fond of me."
"Fond, fond," raged Simon, "I don't want to base my life on fondness. I want love and passion, and that's what I have with Alana, I'm not going ahead with this charade of yours any longer."

"Oh yes you are my boy," Clare growled, "You don't know what I've done for you, for this family," and then said something we couldn't quite catch.

"Quick," said Matt urgently "They're coming out," and with a flash we made it back into the main room of the house just as the door opened and a red face Simon emerged with a serene looking Clare, she had obviously regained her composure, whilst Simon looked subdued and resigned.

Clare glided into the room with Simon following behind, but just as she took a glass of sparkling wine from a tray on the sideboard, lifted it to the assembled guests, and opened her small mouth to raise a toast, Simon turned tail and ran down the hall, out of the house and into his black Mazda Axela, a gift from Cyrus Cargill, and accelerated off at top speed down the track in clouds of swirling grey dust.

A hushed silence filled the room, but Clare seemed impervious to the situation.

"Don't worry everyone," she said unequivocally, "just nerves, he'll be back soon." Then she waltzed into the room and began mingling with the guests as if it was the most natural thing in the world to do.

I froze for a moment as a pair of ice blue eyes set in a familiar face came towards me, but soon realised that the features were arranged ever so slightly differently.

"Meet my dad," exclaimed Matt grasping his father in an earnest hug.

"Hello Martin," I said warmly, "I've been looking forward to meeting you."

"What do you make of all this then dad," said Matt gesturing around him. The room had returned to a happy buzz of chattering conversation with peals of laughter ringing out here and there, and the delightful clink of cut glass upon cut glass. It was the sound of people enjoying themselves. Sarah, dressed in another shapeless concoction, this time in shades of pink, was engaged in what looked like a carefree exchange with her father and Clare over by the open bay window.

"Let's get a little privacy," Martin answered, and Matt and I followed him silently into a side room on the opposite side of the hall to where we had overheard the intriguing snippets of conversation a few moments before.

I decided that I would tell them both about the baby. They listened intently, eyes wide with astonishment, as I relayed how I had found the tiny bones buried beneath the vines.

"Do you think it could be Ailbe?" I said quietly.

"We would need to DNA the bones to establish that," said Martin, "I know someone who could help us."

Matt had previously told me that his father had been a chief superintendent for the Auckland police force. He'd been retired for a few years now, but still had contacts with some of his old work colleagues.

"Let's see what else we can find out?" said Martin, in a business-like tone.

And so we returned to the party.

"Let's get drunk," said Matt.

29.

I wasn't too sure that getting drunk in this house was wise, I didn't want to let down my reserve in front of these people, but there was certainly some good wine on offer so I took another glass that Clare offered me and tried to sip rather than guzzle it. But I was feeling uncomfortable; in fact, everyone in the room except Clare seemed to be uncomfortable. There had initially been some canapés being passed around, tiny wee pastry cases with indeterminate soft fillings and there were crisps and nuts on the table. I was very hungry now and needed something to soak up the alcohol if I was going to continue drinking. I should have eaten more at lunch time; those small bits of cheese on crackers had not been enough to soak up this wine.

Matt and his Dad were chatting away in the corner giving odd stealthy glances around the room. I looked around for Victoria and Clive but could not see them. I wondered if they had left already whilst I had been in conversation with Matt and his dad. What happens I wondered when at an engagement party one half of the couple do an obvious and public runner? I decided to just stand beside Matt and take the lead from what he wanted to do. The more I stood and sipped my wine the more I felt distanced from the odd reality that this party had developed into.

I was experiencing a lost floating feeling that sometimes comes over me in a large crowd, that sense of not belonging, not fitting in was becoming overwhelming. I was still feeling the effects of yesterday's alcohol and I was possessed by the memory that I had seen a thin diaphanous figure by the grave. Victoria assured me that I had been sleeping walking, but I had never done so before. The vision of the figure was becoming very intrusive and I shivered despite the warmth and stuffiness of the room.

When I came to New Zealand it was if a powerful string was pulling me here, it was almost on a whim. To start again, had been the rational thing to do I told myself and others if they asked, but that was not the reason; I had just felt compelled. I had not visited the country before selling up, and heading up in the large Jumbo jet taking me to Auckland, I sat in the plane mid-flight and thought, what am I doing, how did I get here? I had been so tied up with the planning and processing of selling my house and getting my visa that I had missed the fact that I was leaving England. I was worried that my visa would not be granted right up until the last minute due to health issues. My stay in a psychiatric ward could have been a big mark against me. Fortunately, I had persuaded my psychiatrist to write a letter stating that my illness had been brought on by situational events and was not likely to reoccur. I think it helped that I had worked with him in my nursing days.

I had taken a little while to find a property that I wanted but once I saw this one, I purchased it without due diligence and just rushed headlong in.

This last month I had started to feel as if I had been brought here for a special purpose which was why I was putting so much energy into pursuing the wine making idea. But there was something else and I could not put my finger on it. There seemed to be a force that was dragging me along on a path I could not see but could sense.

I started to shake and tried to sit down, Matt realised something was amiss and held on to me.

"What's wrong?" he asked.

I hastily made up an excuse.

"I feel uneasy about the next process with the baby's bones," I whispered, "and I really wanted to talk to Victoria some more before committing to the next steps. I am frightened that exposing what is in that grave will open me up to more threats and possible violence. But I can't see her."

"I haven't seen her for a bit either; let's make our way, out shall we? It looks as if some people have left already," Matt suggested.

"I can't say goodbye to your aunt, I just can't. Can you make an excuse for me and I will wait for you outside?" I hastily muttered.

"Yes, yes of course."

Martin had made his way over to Walter and was deep in conversation as I stepped past him and out of the door. Just outside there was a long wooden bench with a small slatted back. I eased myself down onto its damp surface gulping the air like a landed pike. I was suddenly hyper-vigilant of the things around me; the soft green-white lichen on the seat; the size and texture of the pebbles that were lining the path; the heady pungent smell of the climbing rose adjacent to the window; the texture of the air I was breathing in.

"Hi," said Victoria, "are you OK? Matt said you were looking for me."

"Thank goodness you are here," I said, jolting back into a reality that felt safe.

"I was feeling most peculiar; I think it was the wine. I love you Victoria" I said, "I really love you."

"I know," she said, "come on let's get us home.

30.

I woke up with a jolt. It was early morning and the sharp rays of the sun streaming through a gap in the not quite closed curtains had woken me. I was tucked up in my bed and moving my arm to shield my eyes from the piercing sunshine, realised that I was fully dressed. I had a pounding headache and felt slightly nauseous.

I could hear Victoria on the stairs now, and after a cursory knock she came through the door bearing a mug of steaming coffee.

"By the time Matt and I got you home yesterday you were spark out," Victoria explained. "We really couldn't wake you, so Matt carried you up here and put you to bed – as it were," she added hastily.

"That explains it then," I said, gesturing to my fully clothed body with a chuckle.

"He was really concerned about you," Victoria continued, "I think we can trust him Jenny, don't you?"

Initially I had had my suspicions that Matt may somehow have been involved in the plot to make me leave, and been behind the tricks designed to frighten me into doing just that, but now I knew, without a shadow of a doubt, that I did trust him.

I told Victoria about my meeting with Martin, and the plan to get the bones DNA tested, explaining that I had hoped to talk to her first before committing to what seemed like such an extreme measure, but having not been able to find her, had agreed to Martin's involvement.

Victoria understood at once.

"Oh I'm so glad about this Jenny, to get this mystery solved will be such a relief, it feels like something foreboding is always lurking in the background casting a dark shadow over all the good things you've got going here." She patted my hand gently.

"See you later Darling," adding in a brighter tone, "I've got wine to see to."

She scuttled off down the stairs, just as a sharp pain cleaved through my stomach. I only just made it to the bathroom before projectile vomiting into the sink.

After drinking several large glasses of water I started to feel a little better, and by the time Victoria emerged from the shed at midday, looking like she'd been dragged through a hedge backwards, I had been sick once more, and was now practically back to my normal self.

Victoria was always ravenous after her wine-making endeavours, and we sat down to the quiche that I had made for Sarah's party. The disruption early in the proceedings meant that the food had hardly been touched, so we had brought our contributions back home with us. I had thrown together a mixed salad to accompany it, and we had Victoria's chocolate chestnut tart to follow.

Victoria had been oblivious to the fact that I had thrown up, and now I voiced my suspicions to her that Clare might have doctored my drink with something. She had presented me with my first drink, had come along and handed me a second. She had also tried to deliver a third, but Matt had suggested that we move on to the Te Koko, which he said was one of his most favourite wines. But I had not got as far as tasting that, as by the time Matt returned with the bottle and two glasses, I had come over ill.

Victoria looked alarmed. "How are you feeling now? Do you think you should see a doctor?" she blurted out.

I explained that after I'd been sick and drunk copious amounts of water, I had felt better, but I resolved to tell Matt my concerns when he visited next.

"Tell me about your developments," I said. "How's our project coming along then?"

As we tucked into our lunch, Victoria explained with enthusiasm her progress to date.

For the still red wine, Victoria had lightly crushed the destemmed grapes to break the skins to release some juice, and then cold soaked them for five days to allow for colour and flavour extraction. The primary fermentation followed in the oak vat with twice daily punchdowns to incorporate the cap into the must until the yeasts had converted most of the sugars in the grapes into ethanol and carbon dioxide.

It was a wild yeast ferment, using the natural yeasts present on the grapes, and in the winery, which was what Victoria now called the shed. Victoria was a minimal interventionist winemaker. The wine was now ready for the secondary malolactic fermentation, converting the harsh malic acid like you find in apples, into the softer lactic acid found in milk, and this would also take place in the oak vat.

For the wine destined for the vermouth, Victoria had gently whole bunch pressed the grapes to extract a white juice, then carried out the primary fermentation in the stain-less steel tank. No need for a malolactic fermentation for this she said, "We want a crisp neutral white wine." Once the fermentation was completed, Victoria had filtered the wine and it was now resting back in the steel tank. The next step was to fortify it with a distilled spirit and add the flavourings. I had ordered the brandy eau d'vie that Victoria had asked for and we were waiting for this to arrive, along with the bottles and corks she also needed.

"It's time to choose the botanicals for your vermouth!" said Victoria, biting into a slice of the chocolate chestnut tart with obvious delight.

31.
The Cabbage White butterfly sat nearly motionless on the edge of

the windowsill, its feathery antenna waving gently sensing the vibrations in the room. Amelia was sat at the scrubbed wooden table her head in her hands, she was thirty-six years old and this was the sixth miscarriage she had experienced since Ailbe's disappearance.

Each time she became pregnant she was hopeful that this would be the time she gave Horace the new child he hoped for. After Ailbe's disappearance everything seemed to be spiralling down as if she were sat in the bottom of a deep dark pit. The hole left in them both was clear to see to anyone, but they did not discuss their loss or their hopes for another child, or the absence of children in their life. Talking had become strained and only used for essential communication now.

Each time she missed her period she felt her soul lift as if on the wings of a butterfly until she was ten weeks pregnant, when she joyfully told Horace the wonderful news. Each time she was shattered into pieces when the blood flow started again at elven or twelve weeks. Her Doctor had told her, that it was just misfortune and that there was no reason why she should not become pregnant again. Age was against her now, 36 was old to be having babies.

Amelia had been 27 when they married, and Ailbe was born nine months later. They had named her Ailbe as she had pure white hair which offset her dark blue eyes. Amelia had never been sure if she was Walter or Horace's baby and would have considered an abortion to avoid the constant reminder of her infidelity had an abortion been available to her in New Zealand. Many of her contemporaries had had babies out of wedlock in the 1960's and 1970's; they had gone away for a few months and after childbirth had their babies adopted. This also was not an option available to *her, a newly wedded woman.*

As soon as Walter left her on the eve of her wedding, she regretted her action, he had always held such a pull and control over her, but she could but only blame herself, and Amelia tipped blame on herself in bucket-loads.

After Ailbe's birth in the local hospital Amelia had immediately fallen in love with this tiny replica of herself. She looked so like Amelia that all her concerns disappeared. Ailbe was a beautiful baby who fed and slept well. Horace adored her and when after ten days they returned home from the hospital Amelia was so happy she felt lighter and more buoyant than she had for the previous nine months.

Visitors came and went all heaping delighted adoration on the tiny bundle and praise on Amelia for producing such a beautiful baby. One of the last people to come and visit was Clare. Clare brought with her a tiny present for Ailbe, a pair of hand knitted mittens. Ailbe opened her eyes wide looking straight at Clare. Clare had given a small gasp and lost all the colour in her face. She left quickly telling Amelia that she had forgotten the other part of the gift.

Amelia looked at Ailbe and gasped herself, Ailbe's eyes had turned from a beautiful dark blue like Amelia's to a steely blue, just like Walters. Clare had returned quickly bringing a little kete; a basket made from platted strips of flax leaves for Ailbe, and a small pot containing a cream for Amelia. Amelia opened the kete and saw that it contained a small gold owl attached to a charm bracelet. It is for luck Clare had said intensely looking into Amelia's eyes. And this cream is for you to use to moisturise your skin. She announced she had made it herself.

Amelia had been too busy thinking about Ailbe's change in looks to focus too much on the charm and its inference. As Clare turned and left, Amelia had quickly drifted off into a fitful sleep and did not see Horace enter the room and bend down to kiss the baby. As he stood up a small white butterfly fluttered from the folds of his clothes and landed on Ailbe.

As I sat down to feast on the chestnut tart, I noticed a Southern Blue butterfly flitting backwards and forwards in the window. I rose, opened the window and let it free to fly to the outside where it settled in the rose bushes.

"Do you know what?" I said to Victoria, "It's as if that butterfly is listening to us talk; it does not want to miss out on our vermouth recipe."

We laughed together at the absurdity of it.

"Talking about secrets," Victoria said, "have we settled on a way forward with the baby's bones?"

"I think that we should bite the bullet and just inform the local police. Asking Martin to help could put him in an awkward position with his brother Walter. I feel confident that Matt will support us, but I am concerned after yesterday's odd happening with the possible wine doping of an accelerating risk of harm. If Clare did put something in my wine what might she escalate to if she finds out that we are excavating remains in a grave. It will not be easy to predict what might happen. I can hardly say to the police, 'and by the way I think my neighbour had something to do with it and she is trying to scare me off,' it just sounds so ludicrous."

"I kept the notes," Victoria said.

"Did you? I thought you had thrown them away."

"No, I kept them. They are evidence of threat."

"In that case let's contact the police, explain our concerns, and hope they do a decent job of being discreet."

The phone call was a hard one to make but once done I felt better that we were moving forward, it was a lifting of my heart, and oddly, I did not feel scared.

"Well now that is done let us get our brains into a different mindset; vermouth botanicals," Victoria exclaimed.

"Yes, I have been thinking about this, I would like to make it using local material where possible, what would you advise?" I asked.

Victoria put on her serious far away face and shifting her gaze from mid-distance to my face said "Well ..."

32

On the phone I had informed the police that I had a serious crime to report, but had not gone into details, preferring to relay events face to face.

Now the young policeman sitting on the verandah wore a matter-of-fact face as he nonchalantly jotted down what I told him in his notebook, occasionally raising an amused eyebrow. You could tell he thought I was a madwoman.

But when Victoria showed him the notes his tone changed, and he became more serious. I saved the baby's bones to last, and then Constable Ian Mathews nearly fell off the chair he'd been lazily reclining on.

I had been careful not to directly accuse Clare and Walter of anything, but I made sure I introduced their names at salient moments in my account of what had happened.

"This case is for Homicide," said Constable Mathews, closing his notebook with a snap of his inexperienced fingers. "A detective will be touch, and we'll need to get a forensic team up here as soon as possible."

As Victoria and I watched the young policeman drive off, taking the notes with him, I felt a great surge of relief engulf me, and I knew Victoria felt it too.

Just then, Matt's car pulled into view, and as I waved to him, I realised that he had someone next to him in the passenger seat. With sheer horror I saw it was Clare!

As Matt helped his aunt from the car, he shot me an apologetic look.

"Auntie insisted that I bring her over to see you. She was concerned that you left the party feeling unwell and she wanted to check that you were OK," he said.

Matt didn't know just how ill I'd been, and I hadn't had a chance to tell him about my fears that Clare had tried to poison me yet.

"I'm fine really," I said tightly, and then Clare broke away from Matt's arm and ran over, and up the steps of the verandah arriving in front of me breathing heavily.

Her small face was all concern as she reached out and took my hand, tightly clenching it in a vice-like grip. I felt myself stiffen and tried to pull my hand away, but she held on tightly, smiling sweetly up at me.

"Oh, I'm so glad to hear that," she twittered as I managed to extricate my hand. "I've brought something for you," she continued, reaching deep into the raffia bag that was slung over her left shoulder, and bringing out a little opaque pot, thrust it into my newly released hand.

"What is it?" I muttered, barely able to contain my panic.

"When I met you dear, I noticed that you skin was rather dry, you

English roses aren't used to the intense heat we have over here. I make my own moisturiser so I thought it might be a nice little gift for you. I hope you don't mind, I use it myself, and as you can see … not bad for an old gal," she intoned, proudly patting her dewy cheek.

Victoria snatched the pot from my hand, opened the lid and gave it a suspicious sniff. A delightful smell of marshmallows and pineapple wafted through the still air, leaving an undeniably lovely scent.

"I use feijoa flowers in the recipe," said Clare, in answer to the fragrance.

"What else is in your recipe?" said Victoria, pronouncing "recipe" with clear sarcasm, replacing the lid and setting the pot down on the vernadah table.

"Actually," said Victoria, "the consistency looks a bit gloopy, let me see how well it absorbs?" she continued with a beatific smile, reaching for Clare's arm.

"Oh no dear," said Clare pulling hastily away, "I have a different skin type to Jenny; this one won't suite me at all."

Victoria was about to say something else, but before she could, two more cars drove up and parked abruptly in a line next to Matt's.

A woman in her early forties, wearing a navy trouser suite got out of one, accompanied by a younger sandy-haired man in dark trousers and an opened necked check shirt. They both flicked their badges of identification at us as they approached. Out of the other car emerged two men and a woman in white Tyvek suites, the unmistakable attire of forensic crime team investigators. One of the men opened the boot of the car and started to take out equipment.

"Detective Inspector Maud Andrews," said the woman in a no-nonsense voice, extending a hand, "and this is my colleague Detective Peter Carter."

"Please excuse us," I looked Clare directly in the eye, "but we have a private matter to attend to. Please would you take your aunt back home Matt?"

"Of course, Jenny," he said, and calmly taking Clare's arm he propelled her towards his car. Clare was reluctant to go, and talked to Matt incessantly the whole while, fast words I couldn't catch. As she craned her neck round to try and see what was going on, her face wore a clear look of alarm, and beads of sweat glistened on her smooth forehead.

She was still looking over her shoulder as Matt drove up the road, eyes wide with consternation.

"Where's the body?" said Maud Andrews without emotion.

"I'll show you," said Victoria, and led the forensic team and the two detectives towards Amelia's Hill.

I had been conscious of a white butterfly flitting around the verandah this morning, and now it fluttered off following the crime team towards the vines. I tried to follow its progress, but lost site if it against their white suites.

As I turned towards the door, I noticed that the pot of Clare's cream had vanished from the table.

33.

"Did you pick up the pot of cream?" I asked Victoria hastily once she had returned from showing the police where to find the grave site.

"No," she said, "I assumed you had."

"Blast, it would have been good to have it to send with the

100

police to see what was in it."

"Do you think there was something not right with it?" I questioned.

"Clare seemed incredibly determined to avoid it going on her skin; she looked quite scared," Victoria answered, "I thought that quite telling."

"Mmm, it certainly feels as if we are in the middle of a murder mystery rather than an idyllic vineyard." I mused.

I sat sipping my second cup of coffee looking down the paddock to where the police were working.

Detective Inspector Maud Andrews walked back up to us on the verandah.

"The forensic team may be a while collecting all the evidence, perhaps while they are doing that I can take some background information from you?"

"By all means, come on in," I said, "does your colleague want to come in as well?"

"No that's OK, I have sent him off on other business. He has just lost a baby to cot death, so he is feeling rather fragile around matters such as this."

"Oh," I said, "how sad," suddenly feeling the depth of all my own loses.

"Shall we?" continued D.I. Andrews, flicking open her note-book.

"Would you like a coffee?" I offered. "This could take some time."

"Sure, why not," said the policewoman in ever so slightly a warmer tone.

We all three sat around the kitchen table.

"What can I answer for you Detective Inspector?" I said.

"Please call me Maud."

"OK Maud, fire away."

Her questioning covered the details of my purchase and who had been the previous owners of the property. I answered her as best I could supplying details about Horace.

"Do you have his forwarding address?" Maud enquired.

"Yes, I do, I will find it for you." I walked out to the hallway where I had a small bureau where I kept all my correspondence. I opened the top drawer, the oak squeaking slightly as it caught on the side rail. The bureau had belonged to my great-aunt, and I lovingly kept it polished, but it had warped during the shipping process and it wasn't quite aligned. I looked down at the half open drawer and saw the paper with Horace's address on it. I extended my hand to pick it up and then withdrew it empty.

"Sorry I don't seem to be able to find it," I said returning to the kitchen, "I will look later."

Victoria looked at me and said,

"I thought it was in that drawer."

I shot her a warning glance my eyebrows rising upwards like two inverted teacups.

"No, no it's not there," I said. "I'm sure I will find it later."

Maud looked distracted and unfocussed, as if she were struggling to understand the dynamics in the room.

I asked if there was anything else, she needed to know.

"We will need to investigate the threatening messages you received," she said.

"Is there anyone you know who has a grudge against you?"

I shared a quizzical look with Victoria, wondering how much I should say.

I said, "There is no one who should have a grudge as I haven't been here that long and can't think that I have done anything to annoy anyone, but I can't help feel that it's someone from over there." I couldn't bring myself to mention the Pharaoh name, so I just nodded my head across towards their house.

Victoria interjected, "Will the notes hold any clues; can they do finger printing?"

"It's unlikely given the type of paper that they are written on and where and how you have stored them that they will be of much use, but we will submit them to forensics."

"Once we have more details about the remains, I will get back to you; I may need to ask further questions, once we know how long they have been there."

There was a knock on the door and I rose and answered it. One of the policemen in the Tyvek suites stood there.

"Can I speak to you separately ma'am?" he said.

Maud stood up and followed him outside; they walked off a short distance. We could see them talking and the police officer holding up a small gold object that glinted in the evening light, and then Maud turned around and walked back towards us.

We hastily tried to look as if we had not been watching, scuttling away from the window and attempted to look unflustered as Maud re-entered. She announced, "This might take longer than we thought; it looks as if there is more than one set of bones."

Later that evening after the police had left for the day, having erected a tent over the site and placed tape around the vicinity, Matt rang.

"Sorry about that poor timing earlier. Auntie was insistent that I brought her."

Victoria who was listening in the background said, "Yes, not the best, I could have killed you for your insensitivity."

"It was almost as if Auntie Clare had a second sense and knew that something was afoot," he said, "like a woman possessed."

I had already decided not to tell anyone else about the other bones. Matt clearly did not have any control over his aunt, and I did not want him to know something that she might wheedle out of him.

"I am on my way back up to Auckland now for the next week, but I just wanted to pop back with the jar of moisturising cream that Auntie Clare was trying to give you, somehow it ended up in the foot well of my car. Is now an appropriate time, or shall I leave it until next week?"

Amelia had hung the charm on its bracelet above the baby's crib "for luck" and had used the wonderful cream that Clare had brought for her. Amelia thought that it helped her relax and feel more in control especially when there were increasingly sleepless nights with Ailbe becoming restless and colicky.
Clare visited often bringing more cream with her. Amelia had asked her what was in it. Clare had told her that it was an old recipe handed down to her from her mother, its core ingredients were avocado oil and beeswax she said, with a few herbs thrown in for good measure. Amelia had pestered Clare to tell her what the other herbs were, but Clare said it was an old family secret.

Amelia became more and more dependent on the cream and asked Horace if he could ascertain what was in it. She was beginning to mistrust Clare who seemed to be taking a delight in Ailbe's restlessness and Amelia's fondness for the cream.
Horace's mother had been an herbalist and he had helped her collect specimens for her work. He sniffed the cream in the same way as he did when smelling his wine, closing his eyes and running the smell back and forth through his nose and mouth. He could not be sure of all that was in it, but he could make out the very distinctive smell of gingko biloba and possibly an underlying waft of St John's Wort.

34

I had told Matt to hang on to the cream. I wanted some time to try to make sense of the situation, and I thought that meant making a trip to talk to Horace before the police interviewed him. I told Victoria my plan.

"I see," she said thoughtfully. "That's why you didn't want to give Maud Horace's address; you wanted to get there first. Well, that policewoman seemed like a sharp cookie, you do realise she will be able to ascertain his address without obtaining it from you."

"I know," I nodded. "That's why I will have to go and pay him a visit tomorrow."

The next day, leaving Victoria with her wine-making, I retrieved the address from the sideboard, and drove down the undulating coast road to the picturesque little seaside resort that nestled against the Tasman Sea, not really knowing what I was going to say to Horace when I found him.

He wasn't easy to find, but after asking for directions a couple of times, I found his bungalow at the end of a little bohemian street and pulled up in front just as Horace was exiting his front door with his dog, obviously intending to take her for a walk.

Horace looked a little taken aback when he registered that it was me, but as I got out of the car gave a cheery smile.

"Coming in for a coffee?" he inquired, a smile spreading across his wrinkled weather-beaten face.

"Love to," I replied in an equally cheery voice, giving his dog a pat, "but weren't you just about to walk Mollie?"

"Oh, that can wait; she gets more than her fair share of walks."

And so, I followed Horace into the living room of his modest home, which, although lacking a woman's touch, he'd made cosy and welcoming. As Horace made coffee, he told me he'd thought that moving to the town would be quite a wrench, swopping green wide-open country vistas for sea views, but he had adjusted quickly, easily managing to integrate into the small community. He had even joined a local history group. It had been time to move on he said, and he certainly looked much less care worn than I remembered him, with a spring in his step, and a joviality that wasn't apparent before.

"Oh, I'm so glad," I said with sincerity, and told him all about Victoria and our wine and vermouth projects. About how Victoria had cleaned up all the wine apparatus in the shed and got it working and that as we spoke, pinot noir was bubbling away, working the magic of fermentation. I also told him about finding his bottles of wine, and about the wine-tasting exercise Victoria had conducted.

I didn't mention finding the box. Horace didn't show much interest in the vermouth, but he wanted to know all about the wine in detail.

"You need Victoria to explain about all that," I laughed, "You will have to come and pay us a visit, and she can give you the grand tour."

Horace nodded appreciatively.

Then I told him about what had gone down at Sarah's 30th birthday party as a way of introducing the Pharaohs into the conversation. Horace looked uncomfortable at the very sound of the Pharaoh name, so I decided there was nothing for it than to jump right in with both feet.

I told him about the rat and the malicious notes, and what had happened to Isis, culminating with,

"We found some human remains buried by the vines Horace, they looked like the bones of a baby," I said gently, looking searchingly into his hooded old eyes, but I only stated the remains of one body.

"The police will be in touch with you, but I wanted to talk to you first."

The blood seemed to drain from Horace's face. He opened his mouth, but no words came out. I knew he was thinking about Ailbe, but as far as I knew, he wasn't aware that I was cognizant about her.

I left a respectful silence before blurting out,

"Do you think that is why someone is trying to get me out, frightening me into leaving in case I discovered the bones? Do you think the Pharaoh's have something, anything at all to do with any of this?"

I could tell that Horace was hiding something; he couldn't meet my eyes now or seem to be able to string a sentence together. Finally, he said,

"This has all been quite a shock; it's made me feel very tired. Please, would you mind going now Jenny? I need to rest and process what you've told me, but I promise I will come up and see you after the police have paid a visit."

"Of course," I said getting up and making my way out into the hall. On my way to the door I noticed a delicately carved frame hanging on the wall. To my utter astonishment I saw that it contained three butterflies. They were the same as the ones in the wakahuia box.

35.

I drove home with a great weight of sadness, my shoulders felt as if they were being welded to my ribs. I don't know what I thought Horace would say or why I had felt the need to warn him. Did I think him in some way complicit in the death of Ailbe or had I just not wanted him to be scared by the police turning up. I had a tendency to act sometimes on instinct rather than on logic. I ought to have waited and thought a bit more before rushing off, after all the bones may have had nothing to do with him and Amelia at all.

When I arrived home, it was just before lunch and the house was empty. I assumed that Victoria was still head down, bum up working in the winery. I walked down listening to the overwhelming noise of the cicadas yelling their swan songs urgently as if there would never be another day.

I called out to Victoria and made her jump, she turned towards me her usually immaculate make up a mess, tears flowing down her face. I was startled. I had only once before seen Victoria cry and that was when her son was ill, and she had been told he was not likely to live. Her mascara ran in brown rivulets down her face like peaty streams mixed with treacle.

"What is it?" I cried out running towards her enveloping her in my arms.

She momentarily shrugged me off, never one for shows of affection but then she collapsed into me.

"I don't know what is wrong, I started working in here and thinking about Horace and Amelia and suddenly I was just overwhelmed with this feeling of love and loss. I have tried to work through it, but the feeling became more intense. I imagine them standing in here working together to make this amazing wine and being happy in each other's company but, but there is something that I can't fathom. Who put the butterflies in the box in here, whose bones are they outside? Did Ailbe just disappear?" she gulped and snorted over my arm rubbing her streaming nose on my sleeve.

"Hey this isn't like you at all," I soothed.

"You cry as much as you like, but let's come back up to the house and talk. This place is clearly very emotionally charged for you now. Can you leave what you were doing without it hurting?" I asked.

She nodded and signalled over to the barrels.

"I have more or less finished and the rest can wait." And she started to sob again great heaving soul jerking sobs which intensified as we passed the taped off area where the forensic anthropologist was working.

"Excuse me, how long will it take you to complete this do you think?" I asked one of the officers. He raised his face and said he wasn't sure as it all depended on what they found. I shrugged, that wasn't much help. I was thinking that perhaps Victoria and I should move out for the time being whilst they were doing their examination of the scene, but I had no idea where we could go and the wine making would need overseeing. I could not imagine being able to have a housewarming party after this; that idea would need to go on hold. It's strange the things that go through your mind like wind whistling through a tunnel when you are under pressure.

Once inside I sat Victoria down, got her a cold flannel for her face and a small glass of eau d'vie that I kept for such moments. I wasn't going to have one myself but then I thought what the heck and joined her in a glass. I knocked it straight back, but I had to help Victoria tip hers back; that showed how distressed she was. She gulped and I could almost visibly see the burning effect the drink was having on her. It shocked her back into the present in my kitchen.
"Where did you get this?" she said. "It's good," and then as quickly as she came right, she disappeared back again into a mess of weeping.
"Victoria, tell me what this is about?"
"I don't know," she said, "I feel overwhelmed."
"I can see that," I muttered.
"I heard from Augustus yesterday. He had come into port in Johannesburg and emailed me. It made me realise how much I miss him, how simple and straight forward our life had been until he went off," and again she crumbled into a squat low mess of emotion.
"What shall we do?" I asked. "What do you think would help?"
"More of that eau d'vie," she said quickly. I poured her another and quickly put some cheese crackers and water on

the table for us to eat and drink.

"One of us needs to stay sober," I said. "I wonder if Maud will visit us again today."

We sat together in the lounge for the afternoon neither of us feeling like venturing outside again. The wind had picked up and was whipping the roses against the windowpane, making an irritating tap, tap tapping, as if a demented banshee was trying to get in.

I put that thought to the back of my mind and switched on my Spotify "cruising" play list. The soft gentle tunes from my late teens and early twenties filling the space with memories of a different time, and Annie Lennox, Fleetwood Mac, The Light House Family, M People, Simply Red, and Tracy Chapman intermingled themselves into our reverie.

I told Victoria about Horace's reaction to my visit and that now I was wondering why I had felt so compelled to visit him.

"What if he tells Maud that I went to see him?" I said. "Maud will not trust me or my version of events after this." Victoria was not up to listening or giving advice after her third drink and no food, so I stopped pestering her with my worries.

By mid-afternoon despite the supposedly soothing music I had worked myself into a frenzy of guilt. I had to ring Maud and confess to seeing Horace; so as not to disturb Victoria who was now gently snoring on the sofa: I made my way to the kitchen to use my mobile but as I reached the window seat in the hall a large black and yellow butterfly battered itself against the pane. I dropped my phone in horror; we had been researching butterflies since we found the wakahuia box with them in. A yellow and black butterfly was a harbinger of death.

36.

I was wary over the next couple days whilst the forensic team completed their work with meticulous attention to detail. The investigation was now continuing in the lab.

Maud had visited again and taken some more notes. She made no reference to Horace, and when I said that I had found his address and offered to get it, she waved her hand, saying that Peter had already sourced it. Maud did not say if she or Peter had already interviewed Horace, and her face gave nothing away. She had a penetrating stare which I thought could see right through me, and I felt sure she knew that I had already visited him.

I inquired if there was any luck yet in identifying the bones, but Maud, in her trenchant way had replied that these things take time and information would be shared on a need to know basis. She said she would update me on the salient facts as and when.

Victoria had recovered her usual composure and now bounced into the kitchen, telling me that the fermentation for the red wine had finished, and it was now undergoing an extended maceration, to give it more depth. This was going to be a lush pinot noir Victoria said.

Over morning coffee, I asked her about her feelings for Augustus, and she told me that she really needed to see him and talk things through once his trip ended. From his emails she said it was clear that he was missing her too.

Gingerly I asked her about Clive, which provoked a squeal of laughter.

"Oh Jenny," she said, "Your gaydar never was any good, he's a wonderful guy and I love his company, but he bats for the other side."

We both fell about now, hysterically screaming with laughter, which provided a much-needed outlet for the pent-up emotions of the previous weeks.

We were rolling around in this state when Matt came through the door.

"No wonder you didn't hear me knock," he said in an amused tone.

"Have you been drinking?" This made us laugh even more. Laughing can be infectious, and Matt was unable to stop himself joining in. Before long we were all grasping our sides, aching from the shudders reverberating through our bodies, and now exhausted, fell breathless onto assorted chairs.

"Oh damn," Matt said suddenly "I forgot to bring that pot of moisturiser."

"Is it in a safe place?" I asked casually.

"Well it's in my fridge in Auckland. I thought the heat of the car might make it liquefy. That's where you girls keep such things isn't it – in the fridge," he said pragmatically. Victoria and I exchanged a glance and started to laugh again. The idea of Matt knowing what to do with women's toiletries seemed hilarious.

"I've got something else which might make you smile," Matt continued, "Simon's run off with Alana."

Matt went on to tell us that Simon hadn't returned home since exiting the "engagement party" in such a rage. He'd called his dad a couple of days later to say that he was eloping with Alana.

"I bet Clare soon dragged him back though," I said.

"He rang from Fiji, when he does get back Alana will be Mrs. Pharaoh. Simon rang that day I brought Auntie Clare over, and when we got back Walter told her the news. She is beside herself; I've never seen her so furious, it's like she's haemorrhaging hate."

How's Walter taking it?" I asked.

"Uncle doesn't seem to mind, he says he wants his son to be happy, and that a marriage should be based on reciprocated love, not some arrangement over land."

Whilst Victoria refreshed the coffeepot, I told Matt about the black and yellow butterfly.

"Sounds like a Swallowtail," he said, "You never used to get them in New Zealand, but just recently people have started to spot them over here."

I didn't tell him that the symbolism of its colours had frightened me.

"Any news about the bones?" asked Matt. I told him that I hadn't heard anything and wasn't likely to until all the forensics tests had been completed.

"Dad's keeping an eye on it, don't worry, he's careful, but he knows a few discreet channels of inquiry that he can still access."

I was about to say something to Matt when Victoria came bursting through the door.

"Quick, both of you, come and see this," she shrieked.

She turned and ran back the way she'd come, with Matt and I sprinting after her, coming to a halt outside the winery door, which stood ajar.

On the threshold was another decapitated rat with another note pinned to its bloody corpse. This time it read "No More Chances. You've Been Warned. Leave."

Victoria said that whilst she was in the kitchen she thought she'd seen a shadow pass on the far side of the herb garden, so she went out to investigate, thinking that maybe the police had come back for more questioning, and she shouted out a greeting, wanting to know if they'd like coffee. But when she rounded the corner there was nobody there. Her shouting must have disturbed whoever it was. She said she had shut the door of the shed, so whoever the figure was had the intention of taking the rodent which had been hastily dropped on the threshold, into the winery. "I think they were going to put it in the vat Jenny, to spoil the wine."

37.

"Another dead rat, this isn't making any sense at all. If this is Clare doing these things why would she still be doing it now, now that she must know that we have found those bones?" I said.

"I don't know what she knows," Matt added, "I didn't tell her, but she must have seen the police here and the tarp over the hole, she's not daft."

"No, you are right, so 'who' is behind this, and 'why' are they doing it? Let's put our minds together and throw everything down on a piece of paper. No idea is a stupid idea. You must have done this through some of your work team building exercises?" Victoria said breathlessly.

I went and found an old roll of lining paper and some pens and we sat all three of us in silence as we each scribbled down ideas trying not to look at each other's scribblings. It was hard to get going but once we got started it just snowballed. After ten minutes Victoria called a halt.

"Stop now," she said. "It's time for us to share what we have written down."

"I didn't get past the ideas of the 'why' bit," I said. "I think if we could understand 'why', then the 'who' might follow."

"OK," Victoria said. "What did you come up with then Jenny?"

"Well," I said sheepishly, "These are my ideas. I've sort of started with some core ideas and then widened it up:
Someone hates me personally for reasons unknown.
Someone hates anyone being here, it is not me personally, for reasons unknown.
The next question in my head was why people might do threatening things. How do you have to be in your mind to cut a rat's head off and then threaten someone with it?"

"These are tough questions to answer, I'm not sure we know the answers." Matt mused.

"No, but Maud might know," I said. "The assumption that we have been working on is that someone has something to hide, that they are frightened I might find out about it, but there may well be other reasons. I will contact her later."

"OK, so let's park that question over here on the bit of paper that says "park" then," said Victoria.

"Are we getting a bit technical here?" Matt suggested.

"We need a system," said Victoria huffily.

"What have you put down?" I asked Victoria.

"I have done a lot of the 'who' might have done it," she said. "I thought Clare was the first person, then Walter, Sarah perhaps, even you Matt."

Matt looked on horrified, but I put my hand on his arm so that he didn't stop her in mid flow.

"Then I thought it could be anyone else in this vicinity, in this street, and then the world. What about Frank?"

"What about Frank?" I said.

"Well is there any reason he might be in New Zealand and want you out of here?"

"Oh goodness I don't think so, but you are right we should think broadly."

"Matt, what have you got?"

"Well, I was thinking of the 'why' questions. What might be the reasons someone might go to these lengths. Hiding something sinister came high on my list as well as perhaps some financial gains. Does someone know there is something here that would be worth some money?"

"Like hidden treasure do you mean?" Victoria asked eagerly her eyes lighting up expectantly.

"Well it could be, but what about gold, or silver or some movie mogul wanting to rent this land to film another box office breaker," said Matt.

"Well that certainly opens it up," I said. Just then my phone rang and I saw from the screen that it was Maud.

I answered the phone, quickly trying to put it on speaker so that the others could hear. As I fumbled, I heard Maud saying,

"I need to come and see you and I would like to see you alone, or you could come in here tomorrow." I was taken aback.

"Oh," I said, trying not to sound surprised, "have there been some developments?"

"Well yes, but I need to see you alone."

"OK then I will come to you."

"First thing at 9am," she said briskly. After taking the address of the police station I put the phone down.

"We got half of that," Victoria said. "What do you think is

going on?"

"I don't know," I said shaking, "I really don't know." We packed up our paper and pens and I asked Matt to leave. "OK," he said, "but don't forget I am here if you need me." I wanted to be just with Victoria and my thoughts. It was going to be a long night worrying about why Maud needed to talk to me on my own.

I arose early and showered. I had butterflies in my tummy, and felt sick. I had slept fitfully dreaming of moths getting caught in my hair and dead rats in my bed. I dressed carefully in my smartest black jeans and a loose fitting long merino top in contrasting jade green, my comfort jumper. Matt had texted to wish me luck; I hoped I did not need luck.

Victoria had offered to come in the car with me, but I was only going fifteen kilometres and wanted to be brave enough to do it on my own. I parked outside the police station early, thrumming my fingers on the steering wheel. I was not sure if I could park inside the compound but decided against it, leaving the car instead around the corner in a side street. I felt so pent up with pressured energy that I had to get out of the car and walk to the station even though I was early. It was a typical 70's built concrete building imposing and austere. It was a scary walk up those six wooden steps to the reception area.

Maud came out to greet me wearing black slacks and black blouse; she had her familiar serious look on her face. I tried to be light and carefree, but I was not fooling myself or Maud.

We sat down opposite each other. Maud said,

"Thank you for coming. I wanted to talk to you alone. I will talk to Victoria another time, but for the moment I want to focus on your visit to Horace."

I started to stutter "Well I,"

Maud interjected, "We know that you went to see Horace at home last week. What did you discuss?" I thought it wise to tell all, so I proceeded in telling her about the conversation I had had with Horace.

"And how was he when you left him?" she asked.

"He asked me to leave and was very thoughtful; he said he needed time to think."

"We went to visit him again yesterday to follow up on our previous questioning," she said. "And I need to tell you that we found him dead on the floor."

38.

Completely stunned, all I could do was stare at Maud. A great surge of sadness came over me. Had I in some way caused Horace's death by my visit?

"Did Horace die from natural causes, or was it, was it murder?" I stammered, then more urgently, "Oh my god – am I a murder suspect?"

Maud stared coolly at me for a few seconds, that piercing look seemingly infiltrating my brain. Then she remarked in an equally cool tone,

"The reasons for Horace's death are confidential for now, whilst forensics do their bit, but luckily for you the art of curtain twitching is very much a daily pastime in that little enclave, and someone saw you leave. They clearly saw Horace at the end of the hallway looking alive and well when you exited his home, so no, you are not a murder suspect," she said, momentarily looking down and shuffling her notes.

"I would ask you though to let the police conduct their own investigations in future," she continued, raising her eyes to meet mine with her dispassionate stare.

Then she went straight for the jugular.

"Why did you buy that property Jenny? What made you come all the way over to the other side of the world, to a country you had never visited before, to buy a place you had never seen before, that you say you knew nothing about?" asked Maud.

"I've told you that before, what is this all about?" I gasped.

"There's an old rumour that's recently surfaced; that a vein of gold runs through your land, and I wondered if that had anything to do with your purchase?" She looked at me closely, waiting for my answer.

"No, no, I absolutely did not know that when I bought the property and this is the first time I've heard of it since I've been here. Where did you get that information from?" I said indignantly.

Changing tack, Maud then asked,

"Did you know about the disappearance of Ailbe Mackay?"

"Yes, Matt Pharaoh told me about that," I answered truthfully.

"That will be all for now," Maud said, suddenly standing up, "but I will have some more questions for you in due course, so don't leave the country," she added flatly.

"That's ironic," I almost laughed, "someone is trying to get me to leave, and you're' telling me stay put."

A wry smile momentarily played at the corner of Maud's mouth.

"I'll see you out," she concluded.

As I walked round the corner, I saw that someone had keyed my car. I swore and looked desperately around, but the little side street was deserted. Swearing again I got in and drove directly home, trying to process what had just transpired. My brain so overloaded with questions that felt like it was about to explode. When I pulled into my driveway, I saw Matt's car parked outside, and he and Victoria were sitting on the porch drinking coffee. Without preamble I plonked down on one of the rattan chairs and told them both all about my interview with Maud.

"Oh no," cried Victoria, "why on earth would anyone do that to dear old Horace?" a waver in her usually unfaltering voice.

"I wonder if he was really dear old Horace Mackay?" queried Matt.

"What do you mean?" Victoria and I both shrieked in unison.

"I went to see dad again yesterday," Matt said, and went on to tell us that Martin had been conducting his own surreptitious investigations. Apparently, the curtain twitching brigade was as much alive decades ago as it was now. On the afternoon of Ailbe's disappearance Walter was seen paying a visit to the Mackay's home. Amelia was out at the time. Raised voices, and the sound of things breaking were heard. Walter left looking like he'd been in a fight with blood streaming from his nose, and Horace looked equally dishevelled. Ailbe was clearly seen in the background when Walter left, but when Amelia returned home roughly an hour later, Horace was in a hysterical state saying that she'd disappeared. So Ailbe vanished in that hour between Walter leaving and Amelia returning home.

"Are you suggesting that Horace had something to do with Ailbe's disappearance?" I asked incredulously.

"Let's just say that at the time dad had his suspicions," said Matt.

"Did you know about the gold?" I challenged.

"That was also something that I was going to tell you about today," said Matt. "Dad told me that gossip about gold has begun to circulate locally, but back then there was also a rumour about a possible vein running through the Mackay's land. Nothing came of it then though. Horace started to seriously investigate it before Ailbe vanished, but he maintained he'd drawn a blank, and dad said that he never pursued it after her disappearance."

All the while during this taut conversation a white butterfly had been fluttering backwards and forwards between the verandah and the vines.

39.

It seemed as if time passed in slow motion. No news from the police, and no more threatening notes or dead animals. For the next week Victoria and I spent our days overseeing the wine production and grinding through what amounted to a daily routine.

I think we were both waiting expectantly for news from the police. Matt was back up in Auckland getting on with his life whilst I felt mine was in suspended animation. Usually someone with a good appetite I now hardly ate. Victoria made me all sorts of tempting morsels to eat; I would take a mouthful and feel as if I would choke. I was refusing to go into town as I felt sure that people would be talking about me behind my back, so Victoria was using my car now to go into town to buy the food that she thought might tempt me, smoked salmon, avocados, kiwi fruit. Although I was not well known here it was a small town and word soon gets about in these communities where normally not much happens. The local paper had run a large and dramatic piece titled, "Bones Found In Shallow Grave On Middle-Aged English Woman's Property."

I slept fitfully and no amount of self-talk would persuade my brain in the middle of the night that I would come through this and all would be fine. The monsters of catastrophising took over, wending their way into my overloaded brain. The only thing that stopped me overthinking at night was to listen to podcasts. I longed for the familiar, so I listened to endless podcasts of Desert Island Discs, drifting in and out of sleep all night long. When I awoke in the morning I felt as if someone had hit me with a large cauliflower around the head and that I was wading through a trough full of treacle.

When the forensic team left, the hole where the bones had been excavated was a gapping reminder of the unfolding horror. I was no longer sure I wanted to stay here. What had once felt like an amazing opportunity now seemed cold and forbidding, not helped by the change in weather. With autumn well underway the days were shorter and the temperature much cooler. My heart just was not in it anymore. I had lost my joie de vivre.

One evening, just as we were pulling the blinds down to shut out the gathering evening storm, I heard a car pull up on the drive and looking out I saw Maud.

"It's Maud," I shouted through to Victoria.

"I'll get the door," she said.

Victoria ushered Maud in, who stooped to take off her shoes, as they were covered in mud from the drive.

"Don't worry, it's a hard floor it won't hurt," I muttered.

Nothing seemed to matter anymore. We sat around the

table; Victoria busying herself making coffee, although I would have much rather had a gin. Victoria was trying to keep me off the hard stuff until after 5pm.

Little did she know that I had a secret hip flask in my room. Maud looked relaxed, not in her usual dark slacks and shirt but in an oversized jumper and knee length corduroy skirt which oddly put me on edge.

"I have come to update you on two counts, Horace's death and the notes. I am trusting that you will keep all this as confidential information until it is in the public domain?" She looked pointedly backwards and forwards from me to Victoria.

"It would appear that Horace took his own life."

I gasped, and Victoria let out a muffled cry. Maud continued unperturbed,

"The initial autopsy report indicates an overdose of paracetamol and whisky. The case will go before the coroner."

I was shaking now. "I feel so responsible," I said. Maud looked me straight in the eye, unwavering.

"Why, do you know anything else that you have not told me?" she asked.

"No, I don't think so, it's just I feel so responsible because he was clearly very rattled when I left him," I said thoughtfully.

Victoria said, "Hang on a minute Jenny you weren't the last person to see him, don't you forget the police were there after you, it may well have been something they asked or said."

"Yes, well we will never know that will we," Maud said continuing in her icy tone, "You Jenny, will be called as a witness by the coroner, as will we."

"On the other matter of the notes we have had them looked at by a handwriting expert who says that it is unlikely that they were all written by the same hand. The writing on the first and third note was in blood and the second in red paint. There may be similarities between the first and the last, but it's inconclusive. So, we are not much further forward with that.

The full forensic report on the bones will not be available for some while yet but I can tell you that there were bones of two infants. It would not be right for us to speculate on their origins so please do not discuss this with anyone else."

Maud stood up to go. Then she turned and said over her shoulder, "This will be the last you see of me. I am leaving the force as of tomorrow. Detective Peter Carter will take over the case."

Horace had always hoped for another child but after Ailbe's disappearance the issue became tangled in his and Amelia's differing views of replacing Ailbe.

It had been clear as the little girl reached her first birthday that her likeness to Walter was extraordinarily strong. Those steely blue eyes penetrated his head every time he looked at her. He had mentioned to Amelia that he could see no likeness to himself, but she just brushed his comments off saying many babies do not look like either of their parents. Amelia had become quite cold towards him and had lost all her libido. But a few weeks after Ailbe's disappearance she turned into a woman possessed. She was constantly pestering him for sex, and it was now his turn initially to feel uninterested. His feelings of guilt and horror played on his

*mind making intercourse difficult at first but as time wore on,
he was able to shut his mind to the horrors. Horace had
become pleased with the attention Amelia was giving him but was
not sure if it was him or another child she was wanting.
As the years went by and still no baby, he focussed on the wine
making and shifted back to his childhood hobby of carving and
carpentry, discovering he had a real skill in this area. Amelia
became withdrawn and spent more and more time just
starring into space. He thought that they should move and get
away from the place with so many memories. He had investigated
the possibility of a seam of gold on the property, getting surveyors
out to make an initial assessment. If there was gold, he would have
been able to sell the rights to the mining, keep the winery on but
live on a property in a neighbouring township.
He told Amelia of his plans, but she became so distraught that he
had decided not to mention it to her again. He had settled on
staying and making the best of the winery hoping that with time
she would revert to her previous jovial self.*

40.

Victoria had pressed the pinot noir off its skins, and the wine was
now maturing in two old 250 litre French oak hogsheads, where
she said she wanted it to age for at least three months. The plan
was to try it then and go from there, but she was incredibly
pleased with the way the wine tasted at this stage.

The fancy bottles I had ordered for the vermouth had arrived.
Victoria had been trying, without much success, to pin me down
about the botanicals I wanted to use, but I just couldn't muster up
any enthusiasm with this obscure sombre shadow hanging over
me and my property. Would anyone want to buy anything from

me with the dark history of this place now out in the open?

With her usual confidence Victoria pointed out that that could be its unique selling point, people love intrigue she said, and anyway, the bottom line is always "does it taste good."

"And it will," she said passionately.

Now she sat me down on the sofa wearing her stern face.

"Now Jenny," she began with conviction, then softened her tone. "I know it's hard, and everything is still up in the air and none of us know what the hell is going on, but you can't let that stop you from realising your dream. You think I don't know that you're secretly swigging back gin in your bedroom? Well I do, and it's got to stop. You've put so much into this venture, and it's going well, it really is."

She paused, gauging my response.

"Come on darling, I know you want to use local ingredients for your vermouth, which I think is a master-stroke, and I've been giving it some thought," she hesitated; waiting to see if I was going to engage. When I didn't, she continued,

"So we could try citrus peels from your trees, coriander, thyme and bay from your herb garden, and mānuka honey as a sweetener. Ideally, I think no more than eight botanicals anyway, but I need your help Jenny," she said, emphasising "your" firmly. "What indigenous ingredients could we use? We need something to give a bitter component."

I knew Victoria was right; I couldn't just pack up and leave now when we were just on the threshold of my visions becoming a reality. This is what I had always dreamed of, and this was the place I instinctively knew I wanted to be. My future was somehow inextricably linked to its history, and it was as if had been destined to come here and untangle it.

Victoria's speech about the botanicals had inspired me, and somehow cleared my befuddled brain.

"Well, we could try using koromiko and horopito leaves," I suggested. "They both have bitter flavours."

Although not bitter, I had thought about using feijoa in the recipe, but that had alienated itself by the use in Clare's cream, so I didn't voice that variable.

"Perfect," said Victoria, breathing a sigh of relief, and excitedly went on to say that it would be a work in progress and we would probably end up with quite a few undrinkable offerings before hitting on just the right balance of bitter-sweet flavours that characterise a vermouth.

"I think I will need to extend my stay," she said grinning.

"Fine by me," I said, "I'm not giving up the gin though, I just won't be drinking it in secret anymore," and we both instinctively reached for each other's hands.

"Welcome back," said Victoria.

Gathering the botanicals had been a therapeutic relief, and the final piece in the restoration of my sanity. We picked the tender young leaf tips of koromiko, growing in full sun on the edge of bushland, and made a special trip to the forest to source the horopito leaves.

On our return I gathered the herbs from the garden and picked the citrus, paring the rinds whilst Victoria made syrup with the honey. Then we made up different parcels of varying ingredients. Several small batches of the white pinot noir were brought to the boil with a different combination of botanicals for each batch, and then left to cool and steep. Some marinated in un-boiled wine, and some were left to steep in the brandy eau d'vie, to be combined with wine later.

Just smelling the melange of infusions was an intoxicating delight, and I felt myself return to the world with a grateful acceptance.

Horace was tending his vegetable patch when he heard Amelia's scream, and dropping his hoe rushed into the house and up the stairs with all sorts of things racing through his panicked mind. He found her on the floor of the bathroom holding a bloody bundle in her arms. She looked up at him with desperate eyes.

"I really thought it would be OK this time," she wailed. "It's been 25 weeks, I could feel it kick, oh God, oh God", her voice curdling his brain with its high-pitched bleating.

Gently taking the pathetic bundle from her, tears springing up in his eyes, he turned to leave.

"What are you doing, where are you going?" screeched Amelia.

"To bury it," he said simply. "Don't follow me Millie, it's for the best."

She nodded, silent now with tears cascading down her beautiful face like a waterfall in full flow.

Horace took the bundle out to the edge of the vines; although tears were blurring his vision, he could see that the foetus was a boy.

Peter Carter couldn't be a more different in personality to Maud. He had been promoted to detective chief inspector on her departure, and now he sat on the verandah drinking coffee with Victoria and me, happy to update us on the case.

Forensics had been busy with the DNA samples taken from Walter, Clare, Horace and Amelia's sister who lived on the South Island, and it had been confirmed that one set of bones belonged to a male stillborn baby, a foetal death of around 25 weeks. The mother was Amelia and the father was Horace.

The other bones belonged to a female infant just over a year old. The mother was Amelia, but the father of this child was Walter Pharaoh.

41

Although I had half been expecting this as an outcome, I was stunned by the finality of the findings. My mind felt both clogged, incapable of really processing what we had just been told, and also in free fall, how, who, and why, all over again.

Peter broke into my reverie, "Not that this helps us find out who buried them there, but the field of suspects would be small. Unfortunately, with Horace's untimely death we have lost our main informant. My brain suddenly put on a spurt of action and without thinking I asked,

"Did he leave a note or anything explaining why he had taken his own life?"

"There was a note, but the contents will not be made available until the inquest and even then, might not be disclosed if the coroner decides it is not in the best interests of the family or public interest."

"Has there been any progression on finding out who left the dead rats, and killed Isis?" Victoria asked.

"It is something that we are still looking into," Peter said.

"OK but can you help us get a better understanding of why someone would do this?" Victoria queried.

"Generally speaking the type of person who leave such notes and takes this type of action would fall into two categories. A close family member and that does not seem likely here at all as you do not have any family. Often there will be financial gain for the person doing the threatening; they can be arrogant and think that they are above the law. People can also be criminally insane or have psychopathic tendencies. But equally they can be the most unassuming person, often quiet and undemonstrative.

I did not feel that had moved us on in our understanding. When you see these things on television there are invariably criminal psychologists doing profiling, clearly that is not true in real life New Zealand.

Peter continued, "Rest assured we have ways of discovering who is undertaking such activities. Often there are both DNA indicators and other forensic tell-tale signs."

"Like what?" Victoria asked.

At that moment Matt drove up to the front of the house.

"I have brought the cream back," he said leaping out of the car. He did not see Peter until he was right up on the steps of the verandah.

"Oh gosh," he said, "sorry, I did not realise you had anyone else here with you."

"That is OK," I said. "This is Detective Inspector Peter Carter. He was filling us in on the progress so far with the remains."

"Had you finished with us for today?" I asked Peter.

"I guess so. Please remember everything that I have discussed is confidential, not to be shared with anyone," he said staring firmly at Matt. Matt moved from foot to foot looking somewhat uneasy under this scrutiny.

"It's OK officer, I understand the rules of confidentiality. I am a vet and my father was a policeman," Matt stuttered.

"I'll say goodbye then," Peter had his left foot on the top flight of the steps when I said, "Hang on a minute you might think this very paranoid but could you get this cream analysed for me. It was given to me by someone who I think wishes me harm. Matt has had it in his car and then his fridge, as it ended up in the footwell of his vehicle."

Matt looked from one of us to the other with a look of horrified puzzlement on his face. He started to talk but I shut him down quickly. Peter took the cream from my hand. "What makes you think that?" he said.

"Well, I was very ill after drinking wine at this person's house and they may be invested in either my demise or just making me very uncomfortable."

"Can you tell me who it is?" Peter asked.

"I would rather not at the moment in case it is all just a series of coincidences."

Peter walked towards his car that was parked at the back of the property. And called over his shoulder,

"I'll get this analysed for you and I will be back next week, but if you have any questions do just ask, you have my card."

As soon as Peter was out of earshot whisking himself away up the drive in his car, Matt said, "What on earth is all this cloak and dagger stuff, surely you don't still think Auntie Clare is out to poison you?"

"I just do not know now and this new detective is much more open to ideas and involving us in the discussions," I said, "so I feel more able to confide in him."

"What has happened to the lovely Maud?" asked Matt.

"She has left the force it seems. She didn't tell us why."

I stopped short as I suddenly realised that I didn't know if Matt had heard about Horace and I was very confused about what I could and couldn't discuss.

"You have heard about Horace?" I queried looking intently at his face for how he would react. I carried on quickly, "I wondered if Maud's leaving was in some way connected."

"What do you mean?" asked Victoria.

"Well, whether Horace being found dead after they had interviewed him has raised questions about her behaviour and questioning techniques."

"Why would you think that?" asked Matt. "Dad sent me the link to the piece in the herald about him being found dead at home, do you know more about it?"

I fumbled about trying to remember what I could or couldn't say. The press is not allowed to report suicides in New Zealand so there would be no way that Matt could have found out unless his father had inside information and had told him, but I wasn't getting that feeling from him. I changed the subject.

"Let's go inside, it is getting cold out here and I only have a thin top on, it's so hard this time of year to get the layers right." I prattled on until we were all inside.

"How long are you here for this time?" I asked. "And shall we have a gin?"

"I'm probably here for a couple of weeks now; I have some leave owing so I thought I would take it before the weather gets too bad."

"You are staying next door?" I asked.

"Well yes," Matt looked confused.

"Gin sounds a promising idea." Victoria quickly interrupted,

"Shall we tell Matt about our plans for the botanicals?"

42

Once inside Matt wouldn't let it drop.

"You really think that Auntie Clare tried to poison you at the party Jenny, and that there might be something toxic in that pot of cream?" he said, looking incredulous.

"I'm not sure, but I was certainly extremely ill indeed the morning after the party and I only accepted drinks from Clare. I just had an uneasy feeling about the cream when she was so insistent that it wouldn't suite her skin type when Victoria tried to apply some to her arm, and she looked like she'd seen a ghost when the police arrived."

"She was certainly very edgy during the short drive back, but then as soon as we arrived, she got the news about Simon eloping and rage replaced jittery with a vengeance," said Matt. "She was so agitated that she had to use her GNT spray."

"I don't really know what to think now," he continued. "I will ask dad if he knows anything about Maud though," he added helpfully.

Victoria fetched the gin and concocted three large G&T's, setting them down on the coffee table before us, chunks of ice tinkling invitingly against the sides of the cut glass tumblers. We all reached out for them at the same time, and began to drink with obvious pleasure, not noticing the two butterflies seesawing around outside, one white and one blue.

Matt was intrigued about the vermouth.

"When do I get to taste it?" he inquired gleefully rubbing his hands together.

"Not until we have decided on the right combination of flavours," said Victoria with authority.

Matt looked disappointed, then brightened and told us that his cousin was back from Fiji with Alana, the new Mrs. Simon Pharaoh. The two of them seem blissfully happy, and relieved that their relationship no longer has to be kept a secret. They are living at Alana's flat in town as Clare won't have her in the house and is still spitting feathers.

"Was it so important to Clare that her son marry Sarah?" I asked. "She must have known how Simon felt about her, surely there's more to it than money?"

"Well," said Matt thoughtfully, "the Cargill's are one of the richest and most influential families in New Zealand, but Sarah is no oil painting for sure."

Victoria sniggered when he said that.

Matt went on to say that his aunt was well aware that Simon didn't want to marry Sarah, he didn't love her, and in fact didn't really even like her very much either, but Clare was adamant that none of that mattered, and if he would only just go through with it, then everything would turn out alright in the end.

'Simon confided in me that he thought there might be gold in the surrounding land. At the time when Horace was excavating, Walter also did some drill samples around his property. He drew a blank, but there is a triangle where his land meets the Cargill's and what is your land now, where he thought there was a seam. That parcel of land was going to be part of the marriage settlement if Simon had married Sarah.

The rumour is though that Horace did strike gold here, somewhere over where the vines are, which is not too far from where the land of the three properties meet, but he maintained it was only fool's gold, and abandoned his excavations."

"You might be sitting on a gold mine Jenny!" Victoria shrieked with delight, but continued in a more serious vein, "You don't suppose that Horace knew about the bones and didn't want anyone discovering them do you, so that's why he so abruptly stopped excavating?"

Then I chipped in, "Or someone else knew about them too, and that is why they want to oust me out, and buy my land for themselves? The gold could just be a smoke screen. After all, it costs a lot of money to excavate, so if Horace wasn't convinced there was anything here, it would have been money down the drain to continue."

"One set of bones must be Ailbe's mustn't they?" I was stating what everyone was thinking. "And what was that object the forensic team found. It looked like a chain with some sort of pendent or charm hanging from it. That certainly looked like it was gold, did you know that gold doesn't tarnish – if it's buried it comes out of the ground looking as bright as it did on the day it went into it."

We all pondered on this for a few minutes sipping our drinks, before Victoria piped up, "Clare and Walter aren't on their uppers, though are they? And it's still not clear why your aunt was so insistent that Simon marry Sarah when she knew his heart wasn't in it? That's not the actions of a loving mother. Couldn't some sort of partnership have been entered into with the Cargill's to excavate together? Surely Simon didn't need to marry Sarah for that to happen?"

"Well that's the mystery," replied Matt. "It's true that they are comfortable money wise, but auntie seems obsessed with gold, she even called her spaniel Aurum."

Victoria and I both looked puzzled.

"The Latin word for gold," said Matt.

43

We had another gin and then another mulling over the gold
and reasons for someone wanting me off the land. The
drunker we got the more outlandish the suggestions got.
"Are you staying to eat with us?" I asked Matt. "I thought I
would do some falafel and flat breads. I have the falafel
frozen and it won't take me long to knock up some bread
and humus, are you any good with a blender?"
He laughed, "I don't think I have ever used one."
"Well now is your time to try," I retorted.
Victoria laid the table and got wine glasses out. We were
going to try another of Horace's wines with the meal. I
wasn't sure how I felt about that now that he was dead but
the other two didn't seem pestered by it, so I kept quiet.
The smell of garlic penetrated the kitchen and I was lost in
thought having instructed Matt on the art of using the
blender. He was busy whisking away when I heard a squeal
from the sitting room. Victoria had been surfing the internet
looking for clues to the methods for prospecting for gold.
"My, my," she exclaimed. "This might help us discover how
far either Horace or Walter got with their search for gold.
Apparently, you must register your intentions and get
consent to do the drilling."
"Yes, that's all well and good," I said, "but would they have
done that, or would they just quietly have done it on their
own?"
"I don't think it's that easy to tell if there is gold," Matt said,

"unless they were panning for it. If you are mining, it's not as if you dig down and you can see it, it's quiet a scientific process. In most places that it is mined it is found in quartz veins within volcanic rock. It would be a big undertaking."

"I do not know, I think we may just be barking up the wrong tree, if there is a tree there at all," I said.

We had sat down now, all realising how hungry we were. Victoria had scavenged a selection of green leaves from the garden to make an accompanying salad. We had rocket, mustard leaves, nasturtium leaves, some wild sorrel and fennel; the smell was heady and redolent of some of the best meals I had had in England with Victoria and Augustus, when Victoria would cook up a feast from her back garden.

"It's so good," I exclaimed. "I think that fantastic local olive oil with the lemon juice really makes it."

The wine was a perfect match, and for a moment I felt as if all was well in the world. I snuggled on the sofa whist Matt and Victoria cleared the table.

Victoria started the washing up, shooing Matt out of the kitchen.

"She doesn't trust men with plates," I said. "She would always rather wash up herself than have the worry that someone else might break them. I don't think Augustus ever washed a plate himself."

Matt was looking at me sideways and I became very aware of his presence on the sofa beside me.

"Why are you looking at me like that?" I asked him,

"Did anyone ever tell you that your eyes are beautiful?"

"Not that again," I protested.

"What," he spluttered.

"Well that is so old hat, such a cheesy chat up line."

With that he slid across the sofa, wrapped his arms around me and started kissing my neck softly.

"Are actions better than words; is this a better chat up line?" My body, initially rigid at his touch, was now melting into the sofa like a pot of warm chocolate on the cooker. I felt hot, tingling and ever so sugary as he continued his assault of my senses. Victoria appeared at the door.

"All done," she started, and then looking across, "Oh I see I have interrupted you."

"No, no, it's quite alright," I said, "I think Matt is just…

"I was just going to ask if anyone wanted more wine," she said.

I felt embarrassed and pestered; I didn't really know what I wanted. Matt shot me a piercing look; I still wasn't completely sure about him. I enjoyed his company but still felt like a guilty schoolgirl at his touch.

Matt made his excuses and left quickly saying he would see us tomorrow and, in the meantime, he would talk to his dad. Victoria now took his place on the sofa.

"I have some news," she said looking very grave. "I have been mulling it over for a couple of days; I don't know what to do. Augustus has emailed me; he is in the Cocos Islands and he wants me to join him there."

"I am surprised you are mulling it over," I said. "It was only a couple of days ago you were talking about staying here longer."

"I know," she said, "But he is still my husband."

I felt sad and betrayed. I thought Victoria was all set to stay and help me.

"What has happened for this turn of mind?" I asked.

"Well I can see that you and Matt are getting on so well, I feel that you don't need me now." I looked at Victoria incredulously.

44

Victoria and I both had a fitful sleep, with her worrying about her situation with Augustus, and me worrying about mine with Matt. We could just pass it off as the demon drink, couldn't we?

Just then Victoria came bursting into my room, but this time she didn't do her cursory knock. She just swept in and plonked herself on the end of my bed, her face a picture of misery.

"Oh Jenny," she began, "I'm so, so sorry, it was just when I saw you and Matt together on the sofa last night, I realised just how much I've been missing Augustus. I've been trying to bury my feelings because I was so hurt that he just went off like that. It seems he suffered some sort of midlife crisis after his father died and just had to get away by himself for a while. So, when I got his email moments before finding you and Matt kissing, I became so acutely aware that Augustus wasn't here for me to kiss, that I didn't really think anything through at the time."

She went on to say that, unable to sleep, she had emailed Augustus in the early hours of the morning and asked him to come here after he's done with the Indian Ocean, and he'd replied immediately, agreeing without hesitation.

"I think we can get back together again Jenny, and I think we could make a good life here in New Zealand. I can be a contract winemaker, and of course Augustus can work anywhere with his business."

A surge of relief engulfed me as I reached out to hug her, and we remained like that for a few moments, both with tears of joy running down our cheeks.

Victoria pulled away first with her usual practicality, brushing away her tears purposefully with the back of her hands.

We both began to talk at once, and then started to giggle nervously.

"I can't tell you how happy I am that you've said that," I sputtered. "When do you think Augustus will arrive?"

"In around two weeks," said Victoria. "He's already started to look at properties to rent."

Over the next few days we tasted the vermouth concoctions. Some were unspeakably terrible; some too bitter, and some too sweet. With some the mix of botanicals just didn't work, but with others there were definite possibilities.

We narrowed it down to two possible recipes, but both needed a bit of tweaking. We made another trip to the mountain area to harvest horopito but abandoned the idea of using koromiko. Both citrus rinds would stay, but we would not be so heavy on the orange this time. We threw out the coriander, in favour of the thyme and bay, and we would also try a little mint in a separate batch. So Victoria made up some more mānuka honey syrup, and we repeated the whole palaver again of marinating our selected mixes of botanicals in both eau d'vie and un-boiled wine, and the other process of bringing them to the boil in wine and then letting them steep.

We would need to wait a few more days now before re-tasting. We hadn't spoken about Matt since Victoria had stumbled in to find us kissing that night, but now, as we were sitting on the verandah in the early evening light, she broached the subject.

"Jenny," she began tentatively.

"I know what you are going to say," I broke in, "I don't really know how I feel about Matt. At first I didn't really trust him, but now I can't deny that I feel an attraction," I said tailing off, not really knowing how to continue.

"Well, it certainly looked that way," said Victoria with an impish grin and a raised eyebrow.

"Oh, talk of the devil," she said with clear amusement in her voice as Matt's car purred onto my drive.

"I'll get the gin," she threw over her shoulder as she disappeared into the house with a giggle.

Matt's face was flushed as he came up the steps of the verandah.

"How are you?" he muttered sheepishly, unable to meet my eyes, and sat down awkwardly on one of the rattan chairs.

"Fine," I said, also avoiding eye contact.

"It's amazing what Victoria's G&T's can do."

With that Victoria appeared bearing a tray of the said offenders and Matt and I both laughed an easy reconciled laugh. We looked each other straight in the eye then, held the gaze for a moment, and then looked hastily away again, but the ice had been broken.

"Got some news," said Matt, reaching for a glass. He went on to say that his dad had found out that Maud left the force because she feared that the way she had conducted Horace's interview had tipped him over the edge. Her style is blunt, and she always knew how to wheedle out vulnerability, and then launch a fatal attack; she could destroy a witness's credibility in a heartbeat. Her mother took her own life when Maud was a teenager, based on a rumour that she'd embezzled the post office where she worked. She was innocent. They caught the culprit, but it was too late. Mud sticks and she just couldn't live with shame of losing her job and having people whispering behind her back. Maud never really grieved at the time, and it made her evolve into the hard policewoman who was exceptionally good at her job. The police were the ideal career for her, and she was well respected.

But Horace's death brought all her teenage memories flooding back, and she blamed herself for his death."

"So how did Martin find all this out? He's breaching some serious confidentiality issues here," I said with concern. I didn't want him to get into trouble.

"He's seeing one of the pathologists, the sneaky old devil," replied Matt, "but it's OK, they are both discreet. Anyway, Lucy doesn't know that dad read her notes, and the whole community knows about Maud's mother."

"There's more," Matt continued to tell us that Horace had been serious about prospecting. He was distantly related to James Mackay who in 1857, was the first Gold Warden in New Zealand, so Horace always thought that gold was in his blood. He did register for, and obtain a permit for drilling for gold ore, and drilled for samples at various locations throughout his property.

"Have you ever looked at that area of land I told you about before, where the three properties meet, where the stream runs along, just down from the vines?" he inquired. When I shook my head, he went on to say that one day when Walter was clearing some bush near the boundary he came across Horace poking around, and Horace told him that he intended to prospect for gold ore there. This was before Ailbe disappeared. Nobody had really taken any notice of that area before. Horace was under the impression it was his ground, but Walter thought it was historically Pharaoh land, so there was a dispute over ownership. However, the ensuing investigation proved the land belonged to the Cargill's. It's this portion of land that was going to be in

Simon's marriage contract. Of course, old man Cargill carried on with the excavating, but it was just as Horace had said – the only mineral they found was fool's gold.

Walter never obtained a permit, his drilling was illegal, but when he didn't find anything, he resorted to panning for alluvial gold in the stream instead, again without getting a permit. He used to pan surreptitiously at night.

Although he never admitted it, dad always thought that Walter did find some nuggets this way.

"But the point is, dad concludes that someone either knows, or thinks there is something on that piece of land, that they don't want anyone else finding out about," Matt said.

We were all thinking the same thing and chimed in unison, "The bones!"

"Yes," said Matt. "The question now is who and why?"

Victoria went to refresh our glasses, remarking on the two butterflies chasing each other around the outskirts of the verandah, the blue first following the white, and then the other way around.

"There's one more thing," said Matt. "You were right, that trinket they found with the bones is gold. It's a little bracelet with an owl charm attached to it."

45

"An owl charm, how sweet", I mused.

"I am not so sure it is sweet," Victoria said. "I think owls are meant to be a bad luck omen, they are portends of death."

Clare was sitting in her mother's kitchen wondering how powerful her cream was that she had given Amelia. A white butterfly was slowly moving its wings in the warmth of the sun on the windowsill. Clare had been breeding butterflies keeping them in boxes until they emerged from their chrysalis. She had always wanted children and being of a superstitious nature she hoped that the Small Whites would encourage Walter to marry her so that she could have children before it was too late.

She had immediately recognised Ailbe as Walters's child and it had filled her with hate and loathing. Hate for Amelia and loathing for the baby girl; that girl should have been hers. Her emotions towards Walter were mixed, she had felt betrayed, but it had made her more determined to win him over and marry him. She had spent many years working with herbs and essential oils with her mother and knew that they could be immensely powerful in the right situation. She made her own creams; the ones she used on herself were designed to increase her fertility; the concoction for Amelia was very different; she was hoping that she had the right mix for her; she wanted to make sure that Amelia never had any more children.

She had considered a cream for Walter that would wear him down and make her look more attractive to him, but it was too complicated as he would never think that using a cream was a manly thing. She then turned her thoughts to making an elixir and dropping it into his nightly wine, but that would have been a hit and miss affair as the wine would alter the potency of the mix. She didn't want to poison him.

Clare had taken great delight every time Amelia miscarried; she made sure that she presented Amelia each time with the gift of more cream.

The owl charm she was sure would work in time, she wondered if she might need to hurry it along as she was becoming more and *more distraught at seeing the little girl grow up. When visiting Amelia and playing with Ailbe she had suggested that Ailbe wear the bracelet now as it fitted snuggly around her wrist and looked attractive on her. So from the time that Ailbe was six months old she wore the bracelet day and night.*

Clare watched Ailbe from afar and, whenever she visited Walter, she asked him how the neighbour's family was doing. Walter was always vague. Either Walter didn't know that Ailbe was his child or he did an excellent job of pretending. He never visited the Mackay's and it was clear from the way Horace spoke to Clare when she visited that he wasn't welcome and that she was barely tolerated. One day when Ailbe was nearly one Clare was passing the gate of Horace and Amelia's house. She had just seen Amelia driving into town and she heard a row coming from inside the property. It sounded like Horace and Walter fighting. Creeping closer to listen she head swearing and crashing, but also out of the corner of her eye she saw that Ailbe was in her playpen in the garden. Without thinking Clare rushed in, picked up the child who immediately started crying and ran across the paddocks. She had no idea what she was doing or why, she just ran, and the more she ran the more Ailbe cried.

I decided that I wanted to look down on the edge of the property by the stream where Matt said the contested area was.

"Shall we go and explore that area down the bottom?" I asked.

"Well we can but not now," Matt and Victoria said in unison.

"It's getting dark we won't see anything any way," Matt

added. "Let's go down tomorrow and look."

I was up bright and early. I still couldn't make sense of the theory that the reason I was being scared was because of the bones.

It made no sense that the threats had continued after their discovery.

I was still holding on to the idea that there was another reason.

The day was damp and overcast. Matt joined us just after 9am as arranged, and we walked slowly down the paddocks looking for mushrooms as we went. I have always loved the delight of finding the white tops of field mushrooms poking through the damp grass; it seemed like nature at her most amazing.

When we got to the bottom corner by the stream, without any mushrooms, not wet enough yet I supposed, there was nothing special to see. It looked like the other areas on the property with the exception of a triangle of barbed wire fences. The stream ran quickly here as it dropped down through the barren rock-strewn gulley. Dragon flies still flitted from leaf to leaf and the wasps were in abundance.

We all looked at each other. Victoria voiced what we were all thinking,

"Nothing much to see here."

"No but what is that smell?" I quizzed.

"What smell?" Matt replied.

"That cloying, heavy dead animal smell. You must be able to smell it."

Victoria's nostrils flared, her sense of smell was very acute. It was one of the reasons she was such a good vintner.

"I can smell something," she said. "It's like musk, nuts, and sort of has a dollop of ozone thrown in for good measure." The willow alder and poplar trees swayed in the wind as if taunting us, and I was momentarily mesmerised by the beauty and wildness of my own land. Suddenly there was a loud crashing in the brush below us.

Matt yelled, "Get back, stay behind me."

An exceptionally large and angry wild sow came charging out of the undergrowth.

46

"Just try to keep calm," said Matt. "They only attack if they feel cornered or threatened, just slowly back away."

Victoria and I did as Matt said, carefully putting one foot behind the other as Matt moved backwards with us, his outstretched arms protecting our retreat.

The sow stopped for a moment, the small, deep-set eyes in the disproportionately large head scanning the land before her as she nosed the air with her grizzled snout, her semi-circular lower tusks, much smaller in a female boar, but still eminently threatening, protruding menacingly from her mouth. Suddenly she gave a series of shrill grunts and charged off down the slope towards the stream. Following her path we saw a little humbug stripped piglet drinking from the stream, which now raised its head and squealed in delight. Mother and baby were soon reunited and disappeared together up the far bank of the stream and over Cargill land heading for a coppice of trees.

We all breathed a sigh of relief.

"Didn't she move fast," gasped Victoria.

"They can reach a speed of up to 25 miles an hour," replied Matt.

"And wasn't that piglet cute," Victoria continued in awe.
"Thank goodness we weren't between her and her offspring, that could have turned nasty," answered Matt, "but I think I know what that smell is."
Victoria and I glanced at him expectantly.
"Truffles," he announced. "You may only have fool's gold here Jenny, but you most certainly have black gold."

Clare was in the wood now and her arms were aching. Ailbe was a solid, robust little toddler; Clare was a slight young woman, and her heart condition rendered her breathless whenever she exerted herself. Cries had turned to screaming now, and in an attempt to ease her aching limbs and placate the fractious child Clare sat Ailbe down on the ground, trying to sing a stilted lullaby to her. But just as she did so her ankle twisted over and she fell backwards into a thicket of brambles, hitting her head on an old tree stump that lay half hidden in the undergrowth. She didn't think she'd been out for long, and it only took a few moments to get up and untangle herself, but the crying had stopped, so Clare continued singing, dredging up a nursery rhyme from her childhood.
"Baa baa black sheep, have you any wool, yes sir, yes ..." and then, righting herself, stopped abruptly. To her horror, she saw that Ailbe was no longer sitting on the ground, and Clare just caught site of her blue floral pinafore dress disappearing round the corner of the wood where the path met the road on the way to the Pharaoh homestead. Clare started after Ailbe, but the ricked ankle buckled under her causing her to yell out at the sharp pain it caused, and the injury hindered her panicked pursuit.
Just before she reached the corner the loud shrill of screeching

brakes invaded the air, followed by a piercing scream and an ominous thud, then silence. The nauseating smell of burning breaks lingered in the air as Clare slunk back into the undergrowth, covering her mouth to cover her hysterical sobs; she turned to make her way back home, as a primal cry assaulted her ears.

Horace was still incensed at Walter. How dare he come over here and demand to see Ailbe. It was satisfying that he'd given him a bloody nose though, he hoped it was broken. But Walter's words continued to distress him, could he really be serious about disclosing the truth of Ailbe's parentage? Horace knew that Walter was Ailbe's biological father, he had always known, but his love for Amelia was so strong that he had been prepared to overlook it, even though the truth stared him in the face every single day, he had grown to love the child like his own. Ailbe was such a delight and it was clear that she adored him. When she came running towards him shouting "Papa, Papa," holding her chubby little arms out to be scooped up into his waiting outstretched arms, his heart just melted. And anyway, Amelia and he would have more children, a son to carry on the Mackay name. But he was going to sort this out with Walter once and for all. Horace knew that Ailbe was safe in her playpen and he wouldn't be gone long, as he wanted to get this over before Amelia returned. Jumping into his car he drove out of the drive and turned right towards the Pharaoh homestead. The anger in him seemed to gather pace, accumulating into a burning ball of hatred in the pit of his stomach. His knuckles turned white as he gripped the steering wheel, and he pressed his foot on the accelerator, accelerating more and more as he sped up the road, a red mist of rage blurring his vision. Just as he came round the corner *something shot out of the wood right in front of his car. He tried to break but he was going too fast and he hit whatever it was with a sickening thud.*

He hoped that it might be a young wild boar, the screech he'd heard certainly sounded like it. There were a number of them now living around the area where his ground met the Pharaoh and Cargill land. Wild boar steaks for dinner, he thought brightly as he got out of his car, anticipating the rich flavour of the meat accompanied by a glass of his sumptuous pinot noir. But as he rounded the front of the car his heart missed a beat, and he cried out in horrified anguish. Ailbe's body lay lifeless in the road, a ribbon of vermilion blood flowing from her right ear.

47

"Truffles how exciting, is that area down there mine?"

"It's the area that has been disputed I think, but without checking the land registry I wouldn't be too sure," said Matt.

"I have a copy of the LIM indoors I said."

"The LIM?" Victoria asked.

"The Land Information Memorandum that you apply for when you buy a property. It is prepared by the local council and provides a summary of all the information that all the different departments hold on the property. It shows where things run like pipes and electricity pylons; it would tell you if there were any heritage New Zealand protections against the site, also any permits, consents or requisitions. We could go and get it and come back here to see what's what."

"We do want to make sure that that pig is away from the area before we go poking about Matt advised."

"Well we don't need to poke today, just look," Victoria said.

We traipsed back up to the house feeling light-hearted and excited. I dug out the LIM and we poured over it.

"It doesn't show much at all does it," I said.

"No but maybe we can make more sense of it down by the fence line," Matt said.

Back we went. I had grabbed a small trowel and a trug that I had brought from England with me. Victoria looked at me askance.

"Well you never know what we might find, truffles are very precious."

"I will look later and see what sort of prices they are fetching on the market," Victoria mused.

When we made it to the fence line there was a slight breeze blowing on our backs and the trees were whispering sweet nothings in or ears. We stood at the fence line and really couldn't make head or tail of it.

"Walter must have some details," I said, "because, Matt you said that there had been an earlier dispute and that it was found that some of the land belonged to the Cargill's."

"Yes true," he said, "but I don't know how to raise the subject without him and Auntie Clare becoming suspicious."

"That's a point; perhaps I can give the solicitor a ring tomorrow and see if she can ascertain the boundaries for me." I said.

"In the meantime, let's make the most of this fantastic weather and have a bit of a poke about up here on the path." Victoria suggested.

"I would not know what I was looking for," I said. "I have never seen a truffle in real life. I have had truffle oil and that's about as close as my culinary connection has come to them."

"Do you remember there used to be that fantastic grocer cum delicatessen in Lewes that used to sell them? I remember seeing them in a basket on the counter behind the glass screen," Victoria gushed.

"No, I don't think I ever saw them," I said racking my brain.

"I did when I was in London," said Matt.

"I don't think I ever knew you were in London," I said surprised. Matt looked flustered and Victoria gave him a strange steely stare.

"Yes, but I wasn't there for long. I was on a sabbatical and visited lots of top restaurants, and managed to attend some amazing wine tasting too," he said wistfully and then rapidly his demeanour changed.

"It was just after, just after my fiancé Louise died."

This was the first time that Matt had mentioned Louise. There was an awkward silence, as he didn't know that we knew, but we did know, and I couldn't think what to say. Victoria as always chipped in quickly.

"Oh dear, we did not know that. Were you together long?"

"I would rather not talk about it," Matt choked as he turned his back and started to walk back up towards the house.

We followed sheepishly behind at a distance; he was striding off at such a pace with his long legs carrying him away from us faster than we could catch up.

I tried running but it was mostly up hill and I was quickly out of breath and unable to continue; too much wine and gin I thought.

Victoria said, "Let him go Jenny, it doesn't look as if he

wants to talk."

By the time we reached the house Matt had gone. The happy, full of expectations, atmosphere of earlier had evaporated. I texted Matt and said, when he was ready we were here, and if he felt up to it to come over tomorrow for a further investigation of the truffles. He didn't reply.

"Well I suppose we might as well spend some time seeing how to look for, and pick truffles, and what their market price is," I said.

We were sipping our third gin and tonic, and that was filling our bellies with fire and our heads with fairies.

"Yes we should," said Victoria.

"I shall google it," I said quickly getting my phone out.

"I know this is an odd time to be talking about this," said Victoria looking a bit tentative, "but I have been thinking. I am incredibly happy here and when Augustus sells his boat, we will have lots of money and no ties, I was wondering about buying into the business with you."

I put my phone down and smiled broadly at her.

"That would be so fantastic what a wonderful idea, I was dreading you going back and leaving me here. You have such a talent for the wine making. I would feel lost without you. We could build another house on this land or we could convert the other outbuilding into a dwelling for you."

"Or we could buy another property close by," she said thoughtfully.

"I'll tell you what, while I am on the phone to the solicitors tomorrow, I will make an appointment to go and meet her to draw up an agreement."

Excitement flooded over me. I looked at my phone and a

Herald article said truffles recently fetched $1500 a kilo in New Zealand.

"Oh, wow Victoria look at this, it also says the main season ends at the end of March so we might not find much now in mid-April."

"We don't actually know if they are there or not yet," Victoria said.

"Let's hope I can find some more articles that detail a bit better how to look for them," I said expectantly.

The phone rang, making me jump.

"Sorry for phoning at this late hour," it was Peter Carter. "I keep forgetting to ring you to let you know that I have had the cream analysed, the findings were fairly inconsequential except for a fairly good helping of valerian, some black nightshade and some digitalis."

48

Clare's mind was in turmoil. As she'd made off with Ailbe across the paddock she'd seen Walter's car leaving Horace's place. She'd heard the two of them arguing fiercely and fighting. Walter must have been in such a state that he wasn't concentrating and didn't see Ailbe dashing out into the road.

"Oh, my poor dear Walter," she thought. She knew now that she must protect him; it had been an accident after all, as he would never intentionally do anything to harm his own daughter.

This was all Horace's fault. Clare's resolve strengthened and she turned around and made her way back to the Pharaoh homestead, taking another route from the previous fatal track. She didn't know if Ailbe was dead or alive, but either way Walter would need her help and she would do anything she could and everything in her power to keep him safe. The owl charm had worked, but she hadn't meant it to work like this.

Walter was in the dining room. As soon as he'd arrived back home, he made straight for the cut glass whisky decanter which stood on a silver tray on the rosewood sideboard, surrounded by matching tumblers. That tray was a family heirloom; it had belonged to his grandmother, who had arrived in New Zealand at the turn on of the 20th century, to make a new life. He had been close to her, and she had been proud of him.

"What would you think of me now?" he said ruefully, looking up at the oil painting of a handsome platinum blond woman with pale blue eyes that hung above the sideboard. He poured a large tumbler of whisky and knocked it back in one go. He'd just poured another when he heard footsteps in the hall, and Clare entered the room with a concerned look on her small face. Walter hadn't bothered to clean himself up and Clare gasped when she saw the blood caked around his nose.

Clare rushed towards Walter.

"Oh God Darling, let me see your face, your lovely face," she murmured. "Tell me what happened?"

"No need to fuss Clare," said Walter matter-of-factly, and went on to tell her that he had gone to see Horace Mackay to talk about Ailbe. He wanted to be part of her life. He wanted her to get used to seeing him. He wanted them to get to know each other. He wanted one day for her to know who her true father is. Then he broke down in angry tears.

"But that bastard wouldn't hear a word of it, I just couldn't reason with him," Walter tailed off downing more whisky.

As Clare fetched a bowl of warm water and began to gently clean Walter's face with a clean tea towel, she realised that he wasn't *going to bring her in on what had really happened. By the state he was in she surmised that Ailbe was dead, and that Walter didn't want to compromise her by disclosing any details that might incriminate her. That made her love him more than ever.*

"You know that I would do anything for you, don't you Walter," she crooned as she continued cleaning his face. "Anything at all," she whispered into his ear.

"Yes, yes," he mumbled. "I've got the chickens to see to and some seeds to plant, I need to get on with my chores."

"I'll stay and make you some dinner, shall I?" Clare replied, and without waiting for an answer disappeared into the kitchen, bearing the bowl holding the blood-stained water with her.

Well, if he wants to be all covert that would be fine by her, but she would watch him closely and see what he did with the body. She would need to know what he did with that if she were to protect him.

Horace gathered up Ailbe's lifeless body, engulfing her in his arms, and buried his face in her white hair, sobs reverberating through his bulky frame. He knew what he was going to do. Opening the boot of his car he retrieved the picnic rug that was kept there and carefully wrapped Ailbe in its tartan folds, then gently placed her in the boot.

"I'm so sorry my darling white one, I never meant for this to happen," he muttered, taking an oil rag and shutting the lid of the boot. Horace cleaned the front of the car, scrupulously removing all traces of blood from the fender, and opening the boot again, placed the soiled rag atop of Ailbe's shrouded body. He noticed a road-kill rabbit on the verge of the road, and deftly covered the small patch of blood that wouldn't shift from the tarmac with the

mangled creature. Then Horace got back in his car, turned around and drove home. Once there he parked his car conveniently out of sight inside the old lean-to garage that was joined onto the winery. It was rather ramshackle now, and probably wouldn't last much longer if they had any fierce winds, but it had an interconnecting door to the winery and would serve his purpose nicely. Carefully taking Ailbe's body out of the boot, he placed it inside the cool interior of the stainless-steel wine vat, which would be empty now until harvest time. He placed a selection of hoses and wine-making paraphernalia on top of the miserable little bundle until it was completely hidden from site. Then feeling like his heart was breaking, Horace went inside his house.

He was barely there five minutes when Amelia's car pulled up outside. Horace rushed yelling from the house as she was opening the boot to get out her groceries, and was holding a box of tinned goods when he hollered, "She's gone, she's gone, I can't find her," running his hands through his already dishevelled hair.

"Who's gone, what are you talking about?" said Amelia looking perplexed.

"Ailbe, she was there one minute, and gone the next, I've searched all around and called her name, but she's just vanished."

Amelia dropped the box she was carrying; the tins rolled down the drive as she put a hand to her mouth to smother her scream.

"She may have just fallen asleep somewhere," said Horace hopefully. "Let's look together, I'll do the winery and Amelia, you search the other sheds, and the house."

It was getting dark now and Amelia and Horace were hoarse from shouting Ailbe's name.

"We'll have to call the police, Horace," croaked Amelia, collapsing onto the verandah steps with exhaustion.

158

The police responded with lightning speed, and Martin Pharaoh was soon sitting in the Mackay's living room taking detailed notes. I'll get a team onto it first thing," said Martin reassuringly, and with that left the distraught couple to disintegrate into each other's arms to sob uncontrollably.

That night Horace stayed up late. As Amelia went up to bed, he told her that he needed to go for a walk to clear his head. Amelia sometimes found it difficult to sleep and the doctor had prescribed sleeping tablets prn. When she took them, they did a good job of knocking her out until morning. Horace suggested Amelia take a tablet, and she needed no persuading. He waited until he was sure she was asleep, and then silently exited the house.

The body was so light in his arms; it was easy to carry along with the spade he'd previously left by the side of the house when he'd finished planting potatoes that day. It was a full moon which helpfully enabled Horace to see where he was going as he made his way down the hill and over the fence onto Pharaoh land.

He was making good time, but then he caught sight of a shadowy figure down by the stream. He could see that it was Walter panning for gold, so engrossed in his work that he was oblivious to anything else around him.

Horace ducked behind a cluster of shrubs and waited until Walter made his way up stream, and disappeared from view, then returned to his journey.

He chose a spot right at the end of the wood where nobody ever visited, and that was where he buried Ailbe.

Sure, enough a team was quickly deployed at the crack of dawn the following day to conduct a thorough search of the area, checking all the out buildings, and places where a toddler might hide. At first they searched the land near to the house. But over the following week all the community joined in, walking in a line through all the fields and woods of neighbouring land, meticulously searching for any clue of Ailbe's whereabouts. The police even used divers to investigate the stream, paying particular attention to where the water was especially deep. Clare joined in the search, but Walter was conspicuous by his absence, saying he had the flu and didn't want to infect anyone else. Martin was confident that no stone had been left unturned, but he never knew about the two young police officers assigned to search the end of the wood on the Pharaoh land that first morning of the search. New to the force, this was an adventure for them, and good-heartedly teasing each other as they combed the wood, they had come across a family of wild boars. The old matriarch sow was presiding over the young mothers as they suckled their piglets. The adolescent males, too young as yet to leave the sounder, were engaged in upturning the soil with their powerful neck muscles to root out insects, their tusks maliciously glinting in the dappled light. The new recruits decided not to risk disturbing them.

Ailbe was never found.

Clare had all but moved in with Walter after Ailbe vanished. He had lived alone in that big old rambling place since his parents died, and it had been left to him and his brother. Walter loved the place where he'd grown up with his parents and grandparents, farming the land that they had farmed, but Martin had no such attachments and was happy for Walter to buy him out.

"You need someone to look after you," Clare had said, and Walter made no attempt to dissuade her. Walter was insistent though that Clare have her own bedroom when she stayed over, but she

didn't mind. She was well on her way to achieving her goal now and was certain that Walter would marry her eventually.

She knew that he left the house most nights, panning for gold he said, and she'd taken to secretly watching him from an upstairs window to see where he went.

She was a little late taking up her usual seat tonight. When Walter left the house she usually instinctively stirred, but this evening she had drunk one too many whiskies with him and had fallen into a deep sleep. Walter had turned to drink after Ailbe vanished, just like he'd done when Amelia married Horace, and she knew he was mourning in silence. He still hadn't shared anything with her regarding Ailbe, but no matter, she was dedicating her life to looking after him and he would thank her in the end.

Clare was just in time to see the figure of a man carrying a bundle down the path to the wood. She knew then that was where Ailbe's grave would be.

The following evening, she made sure that Walter had so many whiskies that there was no chance of him waking and wanting to go panning that night, and surreptitiously dropped a sleeping tablet into his first glass just to be certain. Then, when she could hear Walter snoring soundly in his bed, she made her way down the stairs and out of the house into the moonlight. Taking a spade from the shed she ran down into the woods in the direction she'd seen Walter with the bundle the night before, feeling strangely elated.

She knew the whereabouts where the body would be, now she just had to find it.

It was more difficult that she thought; the landscape of the wood in daylight looked very different under the dark cloak that night threw over it. Just as she was feeling that she would have to

abandon her search for now, and take up where she'd left off
tomorrow night, she saw a patch of fresh earth bathed in a stream
of the moon's silvery light, like a beacon illuminating her quest.
Although Clare was slight, her resolve seemed to give her the
strength of ten men, and she kept digging until she saw a small
piece of tartan fabric. So that's what he'd wrapped her in, funny
that she didn't recognise it. Eventually the body was free from the
earth, and Clare carefully filled in the grave and left it as she found
it. The body seemed much lighter in death than it had in life, she
thought, as she stealthily carried it in its tartan shroud back out of
the woods into the field and over the fence onto Mackay land,
making her way to where the vines were planted.

49

"Well thanks for letting me know. Did the report state what effect it might have?" I asked.

"No, I didn't ask for that," said Peter, "but I can go back and see if they can tell me. I assume as I haven't heard from you that you haven't received any more threats?"

"No, thank goodness."

"OK then, will speak again once I have that further information." Peter spoke quickly, and the phone went dead.

"I think he might be a bit fed up with me," I said to Victoria, "I just want to know what effect that cream might have had."

"Well," she replied, "We can always have a look online and see for ourselves."

"No, I don't think so; it will either confuse or scare me or both. From now on I just will not accept anything from

Clare."

I woke the next morning with my head full of plans. I had dreamt of Victoria, Augustus and I making fine wines, digging for truffles, and living happily ever after. It was a real feel good dream, a pleasant change from some of the more recent nightmares that I had experienced.

It was bright and sunny as I arose and went into the kitchen. Thin shafts of sunlight filtered through the curtains highlighting the dust motes that appeared as fairies. I turned to the kettle to make tea and jumped as I saw Victoria sitting already at the table.

"I didn't hear you get up, you startled me."

"Sorry darling," she replied, "I just couldn't sleep. I had been thinking a lot about our finds yesterday and of your suggestions of buying in with you."

"Yes, it's exciting isn't it," I said.

"Yes, very, but I guess we need to flesh out what you had in mind and think about the pros and cons for all of us."

"Have you spoken to Augustus?" I asked.

"No darling, I have not been able to as he is mid-ocean as we speak, but I will as soon as he gets in touch again."

"What do you think he will make of the idea?"

"Oh, he will love it," Victoria gushed, "You know that he will do anything for me, especially now after all this time apart, he owes me my midlife crisis."

"I will ring the solicitor as soon as the office opens and ask her to look into the boundary issues and set up a meeting for us to draft a business contract. I have so much space and spare buildings here that I would love it if you and Augustus lived on the land. We could call it quid pro quo for your input into the wine. I will get her to change my will at the same time so that you and Augustus will inherit the property, as I have no direct descendants."

"Jenny, are you sure? That's a really big generous offer."

"Not really, it just makes sense to me." I said.

"We must make sure," I said suddenly changing tact, "that we don't tell anyone about the truffles."

"I should have spoken to Matt, but he rushed off so suddenly I didn't get a chance." I checked my phone. Matt still hadn't answered my text.

"Let's have some breakfast," I said, "and then I will ring him."

"How about we start the day with a buck's fizz to celebrate the start of our new business venture? We can have scrambled eggs and smoked salmon on that great rye bread I bought at the market," Victoria suggested.

"I don't have any champagne," I said, "but I do have vodka and tomato juice. I would love a Bloody Mary; I prefer mine very spicy."

"OK, I'll get to it," Victoria said. "Leave it to me."

"Please don't make mine too strong," I instructed, "as I have lots to do today, and you know it's that slippery slope, I don't want to slide down it again."

I looked at the clock.

"Actually, I could ring the solicitor now, she should just be open and that way I won't be slurring my words when I speak to her."

I went upstairs and made the call as I had other ideas as well that I wanted to run past the solicitor before I let Victoria know, just in case it didn't work out.

164

I was on the phone for longer than I thought as the solicitor wanted me to explain a bit more and then I had to email her so that she had it in writing, by the time I had finished I could smell the toast.

I skipped downstairs full of updates for Victoria. I swept into the kitchen about to say,

"Hey, I made the appointment," but she wasn't there. I saw out of the window that she was on her phone with her back towards the house. I called out and she turned, smiled, waved and mouthed "just a minute."

I retrieved the toast from the toaster found my drink and took a heady first gulp. My, that was good; I could drink these all day.

Victoria entered the kitchen smiling.

"It was Sunny," she said, "ringing via face time to see how I was getting on."

"Wonderful," I said. "How is she?"

"Well she's OK, she had good news, and she was ringing to tell me I am going to be a grandma."

"My, how so exciting," I ran and hugged her hard, squashing her so that she yelled to make me stop.

"You're pushing my earrings into my head," she squealed. We have some good news, we have an appointment at the end of the week with the solicitor, 2pm on Friday," I announced.

We had our exquisite breakfast, the Bloody Mary slipping down a treat making me feel the day was going to be brilliant.

I looked out the window to see Matt arriving, and went to greet him.

"Hi," I said, "I'm glad you came."

He still looked a bit crestfallen, but said,

"Well I thought I might as well come and see what we can find with the truffles."

"You haven't told anyone have you?" I asked.

"No, I wasn't in the mood for talking after I left you," he said.

He went to the back of his car and pulled out a shot gun.

"I have borrowed this from Uncle Walter, I thought it better to be safe if we are rummaging around in the under growth. We don't want that wild pig charging at us without some protection."

I looked sideways at him.

"I'm not a great fan of guns, but if you insist."

I told him that I had rung the solicitor to get guidance on the boundaries and that I would know by Friday. I didn't tell him about Victoria and my plans. I wanted to wait until the business deal was all settled.

"We are heading down to the gulley," I shouted in to Victoria, "are you coming?"

"You try and stop me," she said.

I was feeling a bit lightheaded following my Bloody Mary and wondered how much vodka Victoria had put in it.

We headed down the track; the clouds now gathering in the sky behind looking like an intense fluffy pillow that was greying around the edges. I wasn't too sure if it was looking like rain or was going to be just one of those days where the clouds build and then dissipate.

"I know now what we are looking for, not the black Perigord truffles; they are not found growing in the wild in New

Zealand, but the white ones." I showed Matt and Victoria a picture of the Tuber magnatum alba that I had found on the internet so that we would all know what we were looking for.

Victoria said,

"Wow look at that name, it all links back to Ailbe doesn't it and the white butterflies, quite a theme going on here."

"You can find coincidences in everything or anything," I said, "but yes you are right, white is coming up time after time. I am still not too sure where to dig. I guess we could start at where we smelt the smell and saw the pig and split up so that we can cover a wider area."

We arrived at the place where we had seen the pig yesterday and Victoria sniffed the air which made me laugh; she looked a bit like a pig with her eyes closed and her nose up in the air.

"I'm not sure I can smell anything now," she said.

"No, me neither," I said, "but anyway we might as well have a rummage here. I handed out small hand forks and paper bags to Matt and Victoria.

Matt said, "Well I think I will head down to where the sow came out, she might have been foraging and found them there, hence the smell."

Well if you are going down there, I will follow you as you have the gun, I don't want pigs to chase me when I am on my own."

"Good point," said Victoria, following on behind us.

50

"The pig released that unmistakable umami smell yesterday

because she was digging for them, but it's highly unlikely that any of us, even you Victoria with your keen sense of smell, will be able to sniff out where any truffles might be located, that's why people use pigs and dogs," Matt began.

"But truffles need alkaline soil to grow, so I suggest that we look for things that like that type of soil. Keep an eye out for oak, beech, and Australian pine trees," he concluded.

Victoria and I were happy to let Matt lead the way, as we followed in his footsteps. It was a glorious autumn day and the sun was low in the sky with a sprinkling of clouds protecting us from its searching rays. Victoria and I were so deep in conversation about her moving plans that we didn't notice that Matt had come to a standstill, causing us both to bump into his muscular back.

"Look over there you two chatterboxes," said Matt with obvious amusement, pointing to a grove of mature oak trees. "That is where we should start looking; there will be no indication above ground that anything is there, so let's see if we can detect where the pig was digging."

We milled around the majestic oaks in silence now, eyes determinedly scanning the dark earth.

"Look, I screeched excitedly, gesturing at a patch of earth that had clearly been freshly disturbed, and the three of us rushed over and began to carefully, but diligently explore the area with our gardening forks. It wasn't too long before I found something, as the pig had done most of the hard work before it had been disrupted.

"Being mindful that the season is really over, we should only harvest mature truffles, and they should be firm, not soft and spongey," said Matt.

Where I had been scraping away the earth, a cream-coloured,

potato shaped lump, no bigger than a golf ball, now showed itself. We all gasped and stared, feeling like we'd found the hiding place of the Holy Grail.

It was Victoria, with her usual directness, who was the first to break the spell.

"Let's take it back and eat it," she said, eyes glistening with truffle fever.

My mind was working overtime.

"I've got pasta and parmesan and olive oil," I said.

"Perfect," said Victoria. "We can grate the truffle onto that – that's a classic dish that Augustus and I saw on a menu in Piedmont once, but it was prohibitively expensive and I wanted to use the budget on a good bottle of Barolo instead." Matt looked impressed, and none of us needed any persuading, as we bore our prize back home with mouth-watering anticipation.

"I take it I'm invited for dinner?" said Matt hopefully as we entered the house.

"Of course, you are, we couldn't have found it without your help," I retorted.

I began to boil water for the pasta while Victoria procured my largest pan. She was adamant that we needed a large pan and lots of boiling water. I set Matt to grating the cheese, whilst Victoria went to fetch a bottle of wine. She appeared flushed with excitement holding one of Horace's oldest vintages aloft. The wines tertiary characteristics of earth and mushrooms would be the perfect accompaniment she said.

Finally, the pasta was ready. We drained it and tossed it in the best olive oil I had in my larder; a bottle of extra virgin Italian oil from Tuscany that Victoria had brought as part of her welcome hamper. Then we divided the glistening strands of linguine onto three plates, sprinkled on some parmesan, and then Victoria shaved thin slices of the white truffle over the top with intense concentration.

She had already poured the wine and we sat down to this hedonistic feast and began to eat. The only sounds audible were the oohs and aahs of sheer delight. It was culinary nirvana.

Now that Clare was married to Walter, she thought her life was complete. She knew that he would propose if she got pregnant. Walter was always adamant that they practice both the rhythm, and the withdrawal method of sex, so Clare knew that she would never get pregnant that way. Once again, she found her saviour in the whisky bottle. At the times of the month when she was most fertile she made sure that she got Walter sufficiently drunk to not realise that he had cum inside her, and if he did realise, she would reassure him that it wasn't her fertile time.

He was beside himself when she dropped the bombshell that she was expecting his child. There was no way out now. Although it was clear that he wasn't over the moon, she had never known such happiness and truly believed that they would have an idyllic future together, living an Arcadian life on the Pharaoh homestead. Clare gave Walter a son, a son to carry on the Pharaoh name and the fourth generation to farm the Pharaoh land that Walter loved so much. Walter was ecstatic and from that point on, although never demonstrative with his emotions, his attitude changed towards Clare, and he became more loving and appreciative. She was a wonderful mother and skilful housewife, excelling at cooking, cleaning, and sewing. In every way Clare was the perfect wife. And so, having achieved her ultimate goal, life was good for Clare.

But when Walter investigated the land boundaries, hoping to

prove that ground Horace thought was his was actually Pharaoh land; she thought her world might fall apart. A sizable chunk of that contested triangular piece of land turned out to belong not to Walter or Horace, but to the Cargill's, and that included the area of the woods where Alibe had originally been buried.

That night when Clare had exhumed Ailbe's tiny body, she had a hard time pulling it free from the earth as a part of the tartan blanket had caught on something sharp in the soil, and when she reburied it near the vines, she noticed that small fragments of the material had ripped off. Had anything else got left behind? Never mind she thought, she'd made a good job of filling in that grave. Besides, why would anyone ever go down there?

She had to get her hands on that piece of land; she just had to protect Walter. Cyrus Cargill might decide to develop the woodland, he was always developing something, that's how he'd become so wealthy.

Simon was in his twenties now, and one night when there was a full moon Clare was lying awake in bed unable to sleep. She always had difficulty sleeping when there was a full moon. Unwanted memories would infiltrate her utopian dream of life with Walter and Simon with a grim portent. But then Clare had the brainwave. She would orchestrate it that Simon marry Sarah Cargill! They had grown up together and the families were stalwarts of the farming community, both descended from the early settlers in the region. She would arrange it that the woodland be gifted to the Pharaohs as part of the marriage contract - it was the perfect solution!

51

Having now discovered that there were truffles on this piece of land I was very keen to keep it secret until such time as I knew exactly whom that land belonged to. We went on to Google maps and tried to pin drop the exact location of the oak grove but that was not possible, so we all made a trip down to the area again with Matt carrying his gun for protection. We took photos and drew a track on the land map that I had acquired with the purchase of the property. "This way when I meet with the solicitor on Friday I will be able to tell with a fair degree of accuracy if that area belongs to me," I said as we were making our way back up towards the house.

"There is no reason to think that this is the only area with truffles in," Matt commented. "So, don't worry too much if they are not on your land."

As we came into the top paddock, I saw Clare and Walter driving out, they gave a cursory wave.

"How are they doing?" I asked Matt, "since Simon's shotgun marriage."

"It wasn't shotgun," said Matt sharply, "just unexpected. Clare is acting very strangely though; she seems driven and anxious all at the same time. She so often has her head in her herbal remedy books. If you ask me she could do with treating herself to something calming."

"That reminds me, I have not heard back from Peter about the effects that cream might have had," I said.

When we got in Victoria said she would pour us a drink to go with our lunch. I wasn't convinced that I should have wine with lunch at it was becoming a bit of a habit, but I have very little self-control where alcohol is concerned so I didn't voice my reticence .

Matt didn't join us for lunch saying that Walter had asked him to have a look at one of his heifers that was limping, and he wanted to do that as he thought that Walter and Clare were becoming a bit suspicious of the time he was spending with us.

"I don't think Auntie Clare could bear the thought of me having attachments here," he smiled, looking at me meaningfully. I blushed, he had been less familiar with me since telling us of the death of Louise and I was pleased that he seemed to be loosening his tight grip on his self-control again.

We still hadn't mentioned to him our business plans, so I was looking forward to Friday when we would have some firmer details and we could share this secret. I am not good at secrets, they make me anxious.

Friday morning dawned cloudy with a promise of rain and high winds. I asked Victoria over breakfast if she had anything to discuss before we went to the solicitors.

"No, I think we have it all drafted out well and I have discussed it with Augustus, he is fine for me to be the partner and he is happy to be on the side lines."

"That's good, when did you talk to him?" I said.

"Oh, he rang me late last night."

"I didn't hear the phone; it always amazes me what I can sleep through."

"How about we head into town early and have lunch before going to the solicitors?" I suggested. "We haven't done that for ages. There is a new vegetarian whole food place open on Ship Street next to the bank that is meant to do the most amazing wraps. "

"Nothing will compare to that pasta with truffle," said Victoria, "but yes let's give it a go."

We put on our best going into town clothes, well smarter than I normally wear around the property. Victoria, as always, looked stunning in a burnt orange loose top and black jeans. We both threw our waterproof coats in the back of the car as the rain was now lashing it down sending rivulets of water gushing out of the guttering and into the path to the car. As we drove up the lane the water ran off the paddocks across the road, the red soil caught up in the torrent making rivers of muddy red that rushed down the road like a high-powered rocket leaving earth's atmosphere.

"Wow this is some weather," said Victoria

"We might be in for a rough ride," I said. "I forgot to check the weather warnings before we left. In this part of the world we have what are euphemistically called 'weather bombs.' Roads get washed away and landslips block access to areas."

We managed to make our way into town driving carefully.

"Let's hope it eases off whilst we are here," I said.

I was exhausted by the amount of concentration needed to get us here. I was ready for lunch.

True to the rave reviews the lunch was particularly good for the price, well done simple food sourced locally with heaps of different salads. We both chose the feta and roast veg wrap with a salad of beetroot and carrot. Luckily, it wasn't a licensed premise, so I was saved from having to refuse a glass or two of wine.

We stepped out onto the pavement and bumped straight into Peter who was head down heading back to the police station.

"Hi," he said, "I was going to ring you later, can you pop into the police station now?"

"Not right now," I answered. "We are just heading into the solicitors; we will be about an hour I should think."

"OK then. I'm back in at the station for the rest of the afternoon catching up with paperwork. Come to the front desk when you have finished and ask for me and I will come out to see you."

Our conversation was brief as the weather was still throwing all that it could at us, and we were trying unsuccessfully to shelter under the canopy of the shop.

We ran straight to the solicitors across the road, a truly short distance but one that saw us arriving at the reception desk dripping liquid sunshine puddles onto the floor. The receptionist kindly supplied as with towels each, so we managed to stop most of the dripping.

Anahera greeted us warmly and we set about finalising and signing the partnership agreement and locating on the deeds the exact boundaries of the land. Anahera had managed to track down the investigation that had identified which part of the contested land belonged to the Cargill's. She provided me with a copy and a detailed map which I decided I would need to take back and look at in situ with the wooded area in front of me.

She then asked Victoria to leave so that we could discuss the changes to my will.

"You are quite sure about this?" she questioned me. "It's a substantial change at quite short notice."

"Yes, I am very sure. It would otherwise have gone to my siblings, neither of whom would be at all interested in the property or running the winery."

I signed and left with a light heart.

"All done," I said hugging Victoria tightly. "I will just go to the police station now. Do you want to come as well?"

"No," she said, "I'll head back to the car and start the engine. I have got very cold in these wet clothes."

The rain had eased, and I walked as quickly as I could to the station. I asked for Peter at the desk and waited for ten minutes. I too now was starting to shiver. Suddenly just as I thought I would freeze to the chair Peter appeared.

"Come through, come through," he said. "I won't keep you long. I have had the results back from my enquiry about the effects of the cream. The analyst said that the amounts of botanicals in the cream were not big enough to have any major effect. The valerian may have had a slightly sedating effect, the black nightshade has little to no effect if not ingested in substantial amounts and the digitalis was crudely synthesised, so again unlikely to have any effect if absorbed through the skin. He did however note that it was as strange mix of things to find in a skin cream."

"Oh," I said. I wasn't too sure what to think now.

52

The weather had eased up and we drove back home in bright sunlight, discussing the events of the day.

"Well, perhaps it was just a present to help your dry skin Jenny," Victoria mused. "I don't think you should use, eat or drink anything Clare offers you in the future though," she continued, and we both giggled.

We were in high spirits as we pulled up outside the house; I asked

Victoria how the vermouth was coming along.

"That reminds me," she said brightly. "It's time to taste the adapted recipes."

It was a no brainer; the concoction without the mint that had been steeped in the eau d'vie was a clear winner.

"What do we do now?" I asked excitedly.

"We just strain it though muslin and mix it with some of the white pinot noir wine; it's ready to drink straight away. I'll do that and you can organise the glasses Jenny. Use those old fashioned style tumblers from you mum's collection, oh, and get some ice – just one large cube in each glass, but don't add the ice until I tell you," said Victoria, who was in her element.

Whilst Victoria was busy completing her alchemy, I fetched two of the glasses she had requested. Mum's glasses always brought back such vivid memories of happy times back in Sussex. Mum was a great hostess, and there was nothing she liked better than to entertain and give people an enjoyable time. Drinks parties were her speciality, and she prided herself on serving the right drink in the right glass. Victoria had always been impressed with her glass collection. She had got on well with mum – they were both bon viveurs.

I had set the glasses on the coffee table and was waiting for Victoria when Matt's car pulled up outside. I went to greet him. "You're just in time," I yelled. "We're just about to taste our vermouth," and disappeared back indoors to fetch an extra glass. Victoria found Matt and me sitting expectantly side by side on the sofa with glasses in front of us when she sailed in. She was clutching a small decanter which held a pale golden amber liquid. I rushed to fetch the ice, and dutifully placed a large cube in each glass as previously instructed.

She poured the viscous liquid over the ice with the same concentration as she had shaved the truffle over the pasta.

"Shall we?" invited Victoria, and we all reached for a glass.

It was superb, with just the right balance of bitter and sweet flavours that were the hallmark of a good vermouth. The texture was smooth and the liquid delicate, but intense at the same time. It was an elegant drink, delicious and refreshing.

It was wonderful on its own, Victoria was jubilant.

"A good vermouth isn't just a cocktail ingredient, if it's made well it can stand alone as a drink to sip and savour," she said with satisfaction.

"Well, I think you have a winner here," said Matt, sipping his drink with overt pleasure.

"Oh, I forgot, I brought you this to celebrate the truffle finding," he continued, producing a bottle of Pelorus from out of his rucksack. Victoria snatched it from him before I could register an answer.

"Good," she said. "It's still nice and cold, let's try it with the vermouth, we need to see how it tastes in its supporting role with cocktails."

Victoria plundered my drinks cupboard, and mum's glass collection got a good workout that afternoon, as we progressed from a sparkling kir style drink served in her flutes using the Pelorus Matt had brought, through classic martinis presented in the glasses that bore the cocktail's name, to a Collin's style drink served in highball glasses, finally returning to the old fashioned tumblers for a Manhattan, which normally uses a rosso vermouth, but tasted amazing with our bianco style.

We all knew we'd struck liquid gold.

One Story Two Endings

By the time that we had finished tasting the vermouth in all its concoctions, we were fit for nothing other than giggling and talking rubbish. Matt left just after 9pm, walking his way back to the Pharaoh homestead, even he would not risk the short drive.

"I don't think I would get the key in the ignition straight," he said. We watched him winding his way up the drive until he was out of sight.

We moved back inside where the warmth of the late afternoon sun had taken the chill from the sitting room.

"Cosy," I said. "Now that all that rain has passed, it's good to be in in the dry and not stuck out on a road somewhere."

"We have not eaten since lunch," Victoria said, "except for those tiny crackers and olives that we had with the drink."

"No wonder I feel so woozy," I said. I looked in the cupboard but could see nothing that tempted me.

"I need something to soak up all this alcohol before I go to bed," I said, "or I will wake at midnight feeling ravenous."

"How about cheese on toast?" said Victoria.

We were both equally unimpressed with the contents of my larder and fridge.

"Do you know," I said, "I can't be bothered, I'm too tired to cook and then eat."

"Cereal," we both chimed together; so not the most gastronomical feast was had with bran flakes and ice-cold milk.

As we sat crunching and slurping our way through the bowls of cereal, I said through a mouthful,

"You know I reckon Clare wanted to hurt me with that

cream but just didn't have the wherewithal to create a potent concoction."

"I am guessing that it is quite hard to do something like that," said Victoria. "Probably even if you were a pro it would be tricky to get stuff into a cream that would hurt or kill someone."

"Anyway," I slurred, "now I am off to bed, it's been a long day and I am ready to crash."

"I am going to sit up a bit longer," Victoria said. "I think I might be able to make another concoction with that vermouth."

"OK, you always did have more staying power than me. See you in the morning."

"Yes, not too early," she called as I turned to make the stairs. I staggered to the bathroom barely managing to clean my teeth because the sink was swaying across the room as if I were on a ship at sea. I crashed to my room and found the curtains to pull. I glanced out and through my haze of consciousness saw a figure standing at the entrance to the drive. I blinked and looked again but the apparition was gone. Imagination I thought; pissed up imagination. I collapsed on the bed and immediately fell into a deep sleep. I stirred later feeling cold; I attempted to pull the covers over me, a tricky task as I was laying on them. By the time I had worked out which way up I was I was more awake than I wanted to be, but as I pulled the covers up to my ears, I was aware of a murmuring of voices. I braced myself a little more upright in the bed and listened again. I felt as if my ears were as big as an elephant's with the effort that I was putting into listening. I crashed back on the bed deciding that I had imagined it.

It was just getting light when I awoke next, the thin reeds of a watery light making their way through my poorly pulled curtains. My head banged and I felt a bit sick. I tried to ignore both sensations until the urge to vomit overcame my reticence to move. I lunged for the bathroom, just making it to the toilet before a cascade of vomit erupted from my mouth. I lay head against the toilet bowel for the next half an hour as time after time waves of nausea and retching overcame me. Eventually I staggered up pulling myself up on the towel rail and made my way unsteadily back to bed. I slept fitfully until I was awoken by the smell of frying.

"No, no, oh no," my brain said. "Please no."

Victoria bounced into my bedroom.

"Hi," she said, "I know I said not too early, but it is nearly mid-day now. Ah," she said looking at me, "Not too good?"

"No, a bit sick," I said. "I can't blame it on the prawns, my usual excuse, just an excess of wine, vermouth and not enough food, I think."

"Well maybe you will feel better with some food inside of you," she said.

"Do you reckon?"

"Yes, come on, have a shower put some clothes on and come down."

Having done as requested I made it down to the kitchen where the smell of frying set me off again.

"Just going outside for some air," I squawked, rushing for the door. I stood holding myself up against the door jamb taking in huge lungful's of air. I felt a bit like a goldfish thrown out on the ground gasping for its last and final breaths, so hopeless was the exercise. As I stood, eyes shut, breathing as deeply as I had ever done before, I heard a crunch on the gravel and opening my eyes saw that Matt was standing in front of me.

"You OK?" he asked.

"No, how about you?"

"I am fine," he said.

"Must have been the prawns," I replied.

Matt went past me and into the Kitchen. I could hear the dull sounds of him talking to Victoria, not the words just the noise. I was starting to feel a bit better, the soft morning air clearing my senses. I braved going back into the kitchen. Victoria handed me a piece of buttered toast.

"Come on, eat this," she advised.

I took it from her and slumped down into a comfy chair, nibbling at the edge of the toast as delicately as a mouse.

"I am going to take Matt over to the winery to show him how it's all progressing," Victoria said.

"Do you want to come?"

"No thanks, I'll just sit here," I muttered.

She and Matt disappeared out and I shut my eyes hoping that at some point soon I would feel better. I must have dozed off as I started as a phone began ringing. I looked across to the bench and saw that it was Victoria's phone on charge. I picked it up. The display said that it was Augustus, so I answered it.

"Hi Augustus, how are you? When will you be here with us?"

"When will I be there? What do you mean?"

"Victoria said that you would be here in a couple of weeks

sailing your boat over … how long?"

"I've no idea what you are talking about," he said gruffly. "Victoria and I are divorced."

"What," I spluttered. "What do you mean?"

"Exactly what I say, can I talk to her please?"

"She isn't in here at the moment; I'll ask her to ring you back." I dropped the phone back onto the work surface looking at it as if it would answer all my questions.

I sat down stunned and completely dazed not understanding at all what I had just heard. Divorced, they couldn't be divorced. Victoria told me that he was sailing here to be with her. Was he sailing at all? I needed time to think, but just then Victoria and Matt reappeared in the kitchen.

"Hey, you are looking white," Victoria said.

"Yes, yes," I said, and rushed past her up to my room. Sometimes information is hard to digest but it is particularly hard when your brain is already wading through treacle. I lay on the bed curled up in a ball wishing that I could just disappear. If Victoria and Augustus were divorced why had she lied to me? Why not tell me?

I heard Matt leave and shortly after Victoria appeared in my room.

"Augustus has just rung me," she said. "He told me he had spoken to you earlier." I sat up and looked her straight in the eyes.

"Yes, he said you were divorced."

"What," she said laughing. "You know him he likes to have a joke."

"No Victoria he sounded very serious."

"No, no, the reason he rang me back was because he thought that you might have taken him seriously." She seemed sincere and had a light jovial look to her. I somehow was not convinced, but I wanted to be.

"In that case," I said, "when is he coming?"

"He has been delayed by a week, so ten days on Thursday."

"Well that's good," I said. "I will have stern words with him when I see him next, he really scared me."

I still felt grim. Victoria looked at me and said,

"Shall I get you some painkillers?"

"Oh yes please," I replied, "with a large glass of water."

She returned with a couple of unidentifiable tablets and a large glass of sparking water.

"What are these?" I asked holding up the pale blue tablets.

"They are my special, 'I've drunk too much' pills," she said. "Knock them back, they will make you sleep but when you wake up you will feel much better."

I gulped down the tablets with the water.

"Oh ugh, what is in this water?"

"Nothing, it's just carbonated," she said, gently pulling the covers up around my shoulders. My brain decided that enough was enough for one day and I fell into another fitful sleep. I woke up in the early evening. The daylight had already escaped from the sky and the stars were shining brightly; a thin moon rising on the horizon.

Victoria was seated in the cosy chair with a glass of red wine in front of her eating cheese and crackers.

"I'm ravenous," I said. "All I have eaten all day is that piece of toast. I feel as if my stomach is eating itself. I wouldn't have got up at all if it wasn't for the fact I felt so hungry. I am still very sleepy."

"I made some mushroom soup and bread at lunch time; I'll heat it through for you," Victoria offered.

I sat down to a steaming and fragrant bowl of creamy soup. "Where did you get the mushrooms from?" I asked.

"The paddock out the back," Victoria replied, "and down by the pine trees that lead down to the winery."

"I didn't know we had any, I haven't seen them."

"Yes, they were there this morning. I saw them when I took Matt over to the winery."

"Are they field mushrooms?" I asked.

"Yes, and some shaggy parasol mushrooms as well."

"Oh, are they OK to eat? "

"Yes, they are fine."

"Are you sure that's what they are, we are in New Zealand you know, are you sure they are the same?"

Victoria smiled, "Yes, I am very sure that's what they are, and Matt helped me identify them."

I ate the soup, it tasted good and the bread that went with it was fresh with a crispy crust.

"You have been busy in the kitchen again," I said.

"Yes, and looking at the books," Victoria said.

"Where did you find those?" I asked,

"In the desk, you showed them to me the other day."

"Did I? I don't remember."

The next few days passed quickly it was as if I were in a permeant haze. I awoke to be fed by Victoria and when I slept my dreams were weird and vivid. I dreamt that I saw Isis and she was calling to me to come to her. "I can't'," I said. "You are dead I can't come to you."

Brightly coloured butterflies crawled over my skin, tickling me but I was too scared to knock them off as I didn't want to damage them. Wakefulness and sleep blurred into each other for most of the time.

One morning I felt stronger and went downstairs.

"Oh good," Victoria said, "You look better, thank goodness for that."

"How long have I been out of it?" I said struggling to hold myself up by balancing on the back of the kitchen chair.

"About four days," she said.

"Four days, what has been wrong with me?"

"No idea," she said, "You were feverish; a flu perhaps."

"Have you been alright?" I asked.

"Yes, yes fine. Matt has been over helping me in the winery. I've been showing him the ropes."

I said, "I thought that you and Matt were conspiring against me."

Victoria said, smiling warmly, "What on earth would make you think that?"

"Not sure but I thought I heard you saying something like, 'Well we have not managed to poison her, let's try something else,' or something like that."

"Oh, my daft girl, why would I do that, you are my oldest and best friend."

I slumped down and cried into her arms.

Over the next three days my strength returned, and the odd thoughts from my dreamlike state receded. As I rested Victoria and I made plans.

The weather was wet but warm and we enjoyed discussing

our business ideas. We still hadn't investigated if the truffles were on my land, so on the next fine day Victoria suggested that we ask Matt over and go down to the gulley with the map, a measuring tape and some string to map out the boundaries on the ground. Matt arrived with his gun slung over his shoulder.

"You still think those pigs are down there?" I asked.

"You can't be too careful," he said, and I smiled warmly at him taking his arm.

"It's good to see you looking so much better," Matt said. "We were getting worried about you."

The warmth was glorious on our backs as we chatted our way down to the gulley. I felt better that I had in a long while, and my legs responded to the action and stretching, giving me a real bounce in my step.

When we arrived at the approximate spot where we had found the truffles the crickets were making a cacophony of sound that was nearly deafening.

"Did you know," Matt said, "the noise they make is dependent on the temperature; they will soon be quietening down as the year progresses."

"I love the sound," I said. "It reminds me of summer holidays in France."

"People do not like them here. They burrow under the bark of trees and cause lots of damage," Matt said.

"Humph, I still like them," I said shrugging.

I got out the map and the string.

"I should have brought a compass," I said. "I can't make head or tails of this."

Matt took the map from me and said,

"North is marked on the map and that way is roughly north," pointing back up the way we had come. "So," he swivelled the map until it all aligned. "If we all take a piece of string, Victoria you head over that way up the stream, and Jenny you move down there into the far end where the existing fence is, then I can triangulate from you both."

"Really, it's that easy?" I said.

"Well it should be," he said smiling broadly at me. So, Victoria walked away from me and Matt up stream and I headed down into the area that we had found the truffles.

I was crashing through the undergrowth trying to get to the far corner. I pushed under a ponga tree and something large and heavy and furry fell on me. I screamed.

"What's up?" Matt called.

"A bloody dead possum has just fallen on me. It's gross, there are maggots crawling all through its eye sockets." I was shaking; it had startled me so much my heart was pounding.

"It looks as if it's been shot through the head," I said. "How weird, who would have been shooting down here on my land?"

"That is odd," Matt shouted back, "and you would have thought that the swamp falcons would have taken it way and eaten it, they feed a lot on carrion and love dead possums."

I left the possum where it was, pushing further to get to the end of the fence line, smashing through ferns and small thickets of kanuka. The air was suddenly silent, no cricket noise, and no noise from Matt or Victoria.

"Hey, I have got to the fence line," I yelled.

I heard a scuffle and a shout and a loud earth-shattering bang, then silence.

I wondered as l lay there why nothing made sense. Things were dawning on me little by little, dripping into my remaining consciousness like thin wisps of mist clearing across the top of a river. But it was too late; Victoria and Matt had orchestrated this from the start. The dead rats; the threatening notes; killing my beloved Isis; encouraging me to drink lots of alcohol; trying to poison me; all a façade. How much of any of my last months here held any truth, I would never know. My last conscious thought as the blood seeped out of me, was that Victoria would have it all, Matt, the winery, my dream.

"Is she dead?" Victoria asked.

"Oh yes very," said Matt.

"Oh, darling how wonderful."

As I lay on my back looking up at the ceiling of the cabin, I saw what I had never seen before, ET's sister, or at least a good likeness of her.

I had not been here long, just long enough to feel the chill seeping into my bones and a sense of strange distancing that comes when your brain has been otherwise engaged.

ET`s sister pestered me. I should have noticed her before; I wasn't sure if she was laughing at me or just looking on perplexed.

I came to this cabin every morning seeking peace and solitude; I should have seen her before. Was she here yesterday?

As I lay there contemplating, I thought perhaps she could be my friend. She might not be as scary as she looked; in fact through my life I had discovered that quite often people were not what they seemed.

I remembered that tall dark-haired man that I caught a fleeting glance of out of the car window.

Slowly, slowly,
But oh, so suddenly
She was gone.

Slowly, slowly,
The leaves were falling
But oh, so suddenly
Their elegance is gone.

Slowly, slowly,
The daylight is shorter
But oh, so suddenly
The autumn is chill.

Slowly, slowly,
She was no longer with us
But oh, so suddenly
Her last breath was drawn.

POSTSCRIPT

My letter to Jenny, Victoria's story.
Buried with you in your coffin.

I won't bore you with all the details, but I feel I owe you an explanation so here goes …

I met Matt in London at a divine wine tasting at the annual Wine GB event. He was there with some of his English veterinary colleagues who were showing him the delights of the city. I was immediately struck by his stunning good looks, his dark brown hair and hazel eyes. He stood a good head higher than me but didn't tower as some men do. Augustus hadn't accompanied me to this wine tasting, he was feeling unwell and had stayed back in the hotel. I was an invited speaker and was presenting a wine, as always I had researched my wine well. I was showing an Off the Line Hip Rosé 2016 which had a palate of yielding stone fruit and strawberries with a hint of elderflowers. I gave my usual in-depth review and recommended it for summer drinking.

When I finished, I returned to my table and saw Matt approach me. "Hi," he said, "I was impressed with your presentation; you are good at your wines."

"I should be," I replied. "It's what I do for a living."

He laughed easily.

"Can I join you?" he said. "My colleague has returned to the hotel."

We spent the rest of the evening together. I barely heard much of the other presentations, but we did a fair bit of tasting. He had an easy relaxed style; he knew a bit about wines but was happy to let me lead the conversation. He told me that he was over in England for a six month sabbatical following the death of his fiancé, and that his home was the North Island of New Zealand.

"They make some good wine there," I said, "very different in style to the South Island but the intense heat and greater humidity

leads to a, blah, blah, blah …"

As he was not going to be long in England it seemed harmless enough to have a flirtation with him. He was so attractive. We managed to meet up regularly and I showed him some of the local vineyards. He was particularly impressed by the Court Garden

Ditchling vineyard's award winning fizz.

A small light-hearted flirtation lead to a full-on passionate relationship. I was infatuated with him and Augustus found out. I think I had stopped being discrete, almost willing him to discover my secret. He gave me an ultimatum, Matt or him. That was hard but I couldn't give up Matt, so Augustus divorced me. I was left with very little. I moved into the flat in London that Matt had rented for his stay and we were very happy, but in that 'just for the moment space' that only new lovers can occupy. I knew he had to go back to New Zealand. I could accompany him but only on a tourist visa and it all seemed so hard.

You had left for New Zealand in a rush and we hadn't properly said goodbye, I had been too tied up with my deceptive relationship with Matt and hadn't wanted to talk to anyone about it.

You emailed me to tell me that you had followed your dream and bought a rundown vineyard on the North Island and that you wondered if I could come and help you set it up. When I showed Matt the address he yelled with excitement.

"That is the next property to my Auntie Clare and Uncle Walter; they told me that some young English woman had stolen it from them."

"Why did they want it?" I had asked. Matt wasn't too sure but he said that he had heard that in its time it had been a highly rated vineyard and that there was a story that there was gold on it.

So we hatched a plan, I wish I could say that I was led by Matt, but I think I was just led by my desire to fulfil my dreams.

We decided that the best idea would be to scare you off the property and we would take it over, you gifting it to me in your will was just unbelievable good luck…

One Story Two Endings

Clare knew that the best object to attract good luck is gold. One of the densest of all metals, but soft and malleable, it could be beaten so thin as to be transparent and it never tarnishes or corrodes. It was a divine and most remarkable substance and could be used for adornment or medicine; gold is noble and unique, and a currency for luck.

It was also a transitional metal, but not just transitional in its elemental sense, but in the way it could help a soul through its journey to reach the afterlife. That was why she had a clear conscience where Ailbe was concerned. The owl had hastened the child's demise, but the metal would give her everlasting peace, and so Clare felt that she was absolved. She had whispered the correct incantations over the earth when she had buried Ailbe, so that her soul would find fulfilment and would not be left trapped in purgatory to torment Clare and her loved ones.

Every time she was in the vicinity of the vines she was reassured to see a white butterfly hovering around the grave site, but after a few years she was intrigued to see that there was always a blue one accompanying it.

Walter had never even hinted about anything that might incriminate him regarding Ailbe. He had however, shared his not inconsequential panning finds with her, and had several exquisite pieces of jewellery made for Clare, both from his own ideas, but also from the designs she asked for, like the four-leaf clovers.

"You must never tell anyone where the gold comes from Clare," Walter had told her sternly, and she had been happy to reassure him that she would never tell anyone anything about his secrets – emphasising "anything" and "secrets." And so, they had concocted the story that her family had inherited some sizable gold nuggets from the old Karangahake mine where a descendant of Clare's had worked and had shares. This was partially true as a distant relative had indeed worked there, but any gold he may have had was lost in the mists of time. However, as the story was eminently plausible nobody ever questioned it.

She was devastated when the news came that Walter's bid for the Mackay place had been rejected because someone had offered the asking price. Now that English bitch Jenny had moved in, and she and her annoying sidekick Victoria were poking about around the vines. This could jeopardise all she had worked for.

It was easy to catch the rat. She had used a trap rather than poison, as she didn't want to harm her beloved Aurum, and it was also easier than she thought it would be to cut off its head; writing the note in the rodents blood had given her a pleasurable satisfaction. What she hadn't banked on was the stubborn determination that cow had to stay and make a go of the property.

Her nephew had told her about the death of that black cat. The bloody thing used to tease Aurum and set him off barking, but it wasn't her who had orchestrated that's demise, and it was a complete mystery to her who had. Clare had however, caught another rat which she duly decapitated and wrote another note in its blood. This one she planned to secrete in one of the wine vats. "Going to start a wine business, are you?" Clare had muttered to herself.

"Let's see what it tastes like with an added extra!" But she'd been discovered as she was just about to enter the winery and was lucky not to have been caught.

But the mystery remained – who had killed the cat?

Walter had become suspicious of Clare when he couldn't find one of the sharp Japanese knives he used to butcher the wild game he shot, but he had become distracted with preparations for Sarah's party and forgotten all about it.

Clare was driving him nuts with all her party planning and his nerves were becoming frayed with her incessant demands. She was completely driven and wanted every minute detail to be perfect.

The activity that always soothed him was shooting. That was just what he needed to clear his mind; he would see if he could bag a pheasant for the pot.

Aurum was a magnificent gun dog, and he called the animals name as he crossed the yard with his shot gun open over the crook of his arm. Then cursing, he realised he might need some more bullets, and was just about to turn back to the house to get some, when he remembered that he kept a stash locked away in the little shed that adjoined Clare's apothecary. She was always in there busy concocting her creams and potions, but was careful to lock it when not in use – some of the herbs she used could be fatal to animals she said, and she was mindful of the inquisitive Aurum ingesting something that would harm him. Today however, the door was ajar, and he was just in time to see the spaniel's wagging tail disappearing inside.

Calling the dog's name Walter opened the door to find him sniffing around excitedly in the corner of the dark room, his nose snuffling in a piece of sackcloth, making little whining and yelping noises, his tail wagging so hard that it looked like it might spiral off at any second. He was clearly very aroused.

Suddenly Aurum let out an acute yelp. This was not a yelp of excitement; this was a yelp of pain, and he jumped back from the corner with blood pouring from his muzzle.

"There, there boy," crooned Walter, stroking the animal to calm him down. Then he reached to see what had caused the injury. The beige of the sackcloth was now tinged with the red of the dog's blood, and as he gingerly opened the parcel Walter was astonished to find his missing knife.

"What happened to Aurum's nose?" shrieked Clare, as she bent down to examine her beloved pet.

"Must have cut himself on something sharp," replied Walter, eyeing Clare closely.

"I've told you to be careful to make sure there is no loose barbed wire about in the fields," Clare barked. "Looks like quite a nasty cut. I'll get Matt to have a look at it, but you must be more vigilant when you take him shooting."

"I didn't take him today," replied Walter. "Couldn't find him, but when I returned, he was coming out of your apothecary and his nose was bleeding then." He watched Clare's face intently. Walter had actually taken the dog with him, but he didn't want Clare to know that.

She flushed, the blood flow beginning in her neck, and then creeping up until her entire face was bright red.

"What have you done Clare?" snarled Walter grasping her slim shoulders with his big work-worn hands.

And so, Clare told him about the rats. She told Walter that she wanted the property for Simon, who had always wanted to make wine, and that the acquisition would extend the Pharaoh land – the land Walter loved. She said she had been so incensed when an outsider bought the land from right under their noses that she momentarily lost her senses.

196

She said nothing about Ailbe.

Walter made Clare promise that she wouldn't meddle any further, but he felt sure that there was more to her story than she was making out. He had always known about her fascination with herbal potions, and that she had leanings towards the occult. He'd dismissed this as just an interest in folklore she'd inherited from her Irish mother and grandmother before her, but now he was concerned that it might be something more sinister, and he was worried Clare could do something more dire than killing a rat. He had to try and make Jenny leave before anything fatal happened to her.

So, he thought he would follow in Clare's vein and leave another decapitated rat with a malicious note.

Trapping a rat and decapitating it was no problem, and he knew just how to copy Clare's handwriting, picking out the letters "Leave Bitch" in red paint on a scrap of paper torn from a buff envelope. He would leave it round the back of Jenny's shed.

Walter was crouching on the ground. He had taken the bleeding rat out of the plastic bag he'd put it in to protect his rucksack, and was just about to pin the note to its tumefied body when that black cat that was always sitting on the wall of his yard, swishing its tail tantalizing Aurum, came sashaying round the corner.

The cat smelled the blood and came bounding over and was nosing the rat before Walter could prevent it. He tried to shoo the feline away, but she was intent on getting the prize for herself and had got hold of the rodent between her sharp teeth. Walter swiped hard at the cat, sending it flying through the air, landing on the ground with a resounding thump. But the cat it didn't get up again and made no sound. Walter went over to inspect the animal and saw to his horror that it had struck its head on the tip of a sharp piece of chalk that was poking through the ground. That was why the vines did so well on this area of land, it was pure limestone. The stone hadn't penetrated the cat's skin, and there was no blood, but the blow must have been fatal. Panicking now, it was a couple of minutes before Walter realised what he had to do.

Replacing the rat in its plastic protection he returned it to his rucksack and retraced his footsteps home. Clare was out shopping in town. Walter easily picked the lock of the apothecary door. He had always had a knack for picking locks and was soon inside staring at Clare's array of jars and pots, all carefully labelled with their contents. Water knew a thing or two about herbs himself, having developed an interest in it over the years through Clare's obsession. Some of her remedies were useful on the farm and advantageous to know. He knew just what he was after.

Walter was soon back staring down at the cat. It looked like it was sleeping stretched out peacefully on the ground in the sun, but its impossibly pink tongue was protruding from its mouth, and a slight foam had appeared around the edges. He carefully placed a small portion of Aurum's dog food that he'd doctored with tincture of aconite in the cat's mouth, pinned the note to its collar and left the scene with a heavy heart.

He knew that he would never have been able to decapitate the cat. Although it had been a nuisance, he was an animal lover, and actually did like cats. He would have had a couple himself to keep the rats down around the farm if hadn't been for Clare. She couldn't stand them, she thought they were unlucky.

Victoria had made up all the vermouth now and decanted it into the beautiful heavy bottomed square bottles I had ordered for the purpose. I was now in the process of designing a label. I'd always dabbled in painting, finding it an enjoyable and creative way to relax, and some of the results were, if I don't say so myself – not bad at all.

I'd drawn out various ideas but needed to go into town to replenish some painting materials. Victoria said she would come with me as she wanted to check out what vermouths, if any, the liquor shops sold, and how much they were priced at. We were both leaving the house when Matt's car pulled up outside. I told him our plans and said that we shouldn't be long, and he was welcome to stay and wait for us. He could make himself useful and weed the herb garden if he liked. Matt readily accepted the challenge.

"Hang on I'll unlock the door for you, so you can make yourself a coffee," I yelled from the open window of the car, and made to get out.

"Don't worry Jenny, I'll be OK until you return," replied Matt, "then you can make me one as a reward for my services," he grinned. As we drove away, I could see him in the interior mirror emerging from the potting shed with a hoe, trowel and bucket. A shy smile crept across my face.

Victoria noticed.

"So how are you two getting along?" she asked, turning towards me cocking a questioning eyebrow.

"I like him Victoria," I answered truthfully. "I'm just taking it a day at a time and see where things lead," I concluded.

"Might lead back to the sofa," chortled Victoria, and I blushed remembering the night she had caught Matt and I kissing. But a warm feeling had enveloped me, and I felt nothing but contentment as we drove the scenic route to town. It was a lovely crisp autumn morning and the trees were beginning to change colour, throwing yellow, gold and hot orange branches up to an impossibly blue sky.

Matt was busy weeding. He was on his hands and knees exhuming obstinate weeds with the trowel when he heard the car on the drive. Raising himself upright onto his knees, Matt was just about to wave and invite Jenny and Victoria to inspect his mornings work when he saw that the car that had pulled up was not Jenny's. Instead of Jenny's little blue Honda, this was an imposing dark grey Toyota Land Cruiser. Matt quickly ducked back down, trying to hide himself behind the sprawling rosemary bush, and watched clandestinely as a tall dark man with broad shoulders emerged confidently from the car, carrying a large rucksack. He sprinted up the steps of the verandah with equal confidence and tried the handle of the door, and when he realised it was locked began to hammer on it loudly.

When that brought no reply, he stepped back from the door, turned around and surveyed the property with both hands on firm hips. Then seemingly saying something to himself, he leapt down the steps and made for the winery.

Matt was on him in an instant. He had emptied the weeds from the bucket as he dashed towards the man, and now swung it at him just as the intruder turned to see his assailant, catching him across the temple. The man immediately crumpled onto the ground, his large frame blocking the door to the winery, with a purple egg beginning to erupt from his hairline. Just then Jenny's car swung round the corner and parked alongside the Toyota. Victoria leapt screaming from the car.

"What have you done Matt?" she demanded, bending down and

cradling the man's head in her lap. Before Matt could answer the man began to stir.

"Where am I?" he muttered, moving a hand to his temple and wincing.

"Oh Augustus," breathed Victoria with relief. "Are you alright?"

The four of us were sitting on the verandah now, with Augustus holding a flannel filled with ice to his head with one hand and a large glass of brandy in the other. Matt had apologised profusely and was completely embarrassed. He defended himself by saying that as far he was concerned a stranger just turned up out of the blue, bearing a rucksack which was clearly full to bursting, and given the turn of recent events he wasn't going to take any chances. But Matt was mortified and continued to apologise. Augustus lifted his handsome head, grimacing slightly as he did so, and fixed Matt with a pair of cold brown eyes, which had the effect of making Matt start to stutter another apology. Then the cold stare melted into a twinkle, instantly diverting the face into a picture of jovial amusement.

"No worries mate," said Augustus, putting down the ice filled flannel and extending a hand towards Matt. "It's good to know that someone is looking out for them," nodding towards Victoria and me.

Matt grasped Augustus' hand and the two men both laughed their own laughs of relief, keeping the grip for a few moments.

"Well, you could have let us know you were coming," said Victoria, fussing round her husband like a mother hen.

"I wanted to surprise you," Augustus replied.

"Well you certainly did that," I chipped in, and we laughed again, knowing that we were all going to get along just fine.

Augustus told us that he had rented a property about 10 minutes' drive away down the road. I knew the couple who owned it. They were a wealthy pair of Asian entrepreneurs, who spent six months in New Zealand and six months in Malaysia for tax purposes. The house was stunning. Victoria and Matt where going to stay there while they got started on building their own home on my property.

Matt had never made a dessert. He could rustle up a decent basic meal, but baking was in another realm to him. Augustus had brought a bottle of Sauternes with him, knowing that Victoria adored dessert wine, and she had said that it would go perfectly with something lemony. Matt thought that making pastry would be beyond him, but Auntie Clare made these lemon cupcakes that were filled with lemon curd and had an elderflower mascarpone icing. Everyone that tasted them raved about how good they were, and she said the recipe was a doddle. He was sure that he could knock up a batch of those, and whilst he was staying with her, Clare had said that he could have free rein of her kitchen. "Use anything that's there," she had said.

Matt had dutifully bought all the ingredients from town that Clare didn't already have and followed her recipe to a T. Victoria would approve of that he thought, smiling to himself as he took the cakes out of the oven. They had risen perfectly, and a mouth-watering smell of sweet buttery notes tinged with citrus filed the kitchen.

Whilst they were cooling Matt made the icing, creaming the mascarpone cheese with icing sugar and elderflower cordial. Dipping an index finger into the mix, he licked it tentatively, and then sighed with delight – it tasted heavenly.

The cakes were cool now and with meticulous care Matt made a little hole in the top of each one, filling them with lemon curd. He had bought the best home-made curd he could find, and it hadn't been cheap. Finally, he placed a good amount of icing on top of the cakes and swirled it around to cover them completely.

One was a bit wonky, so he put that on a plate for Auntie Clare to try. At that moment she came in and approvingly surveyed the scene before her. When Matt indicated the cake to her she smiled broadly and told him she would have it later with a cup of coffee. She told him that Walter needed help with some fencing, and not to worry about the cakes; she would put them in a Tupperware container for him, so that he could transport them over to Jenny's place later. Thanking her warmly Matt went out to help his uncle. The broad smile Clare wore became broader, and a deranged glint filled her eyes. She knew what she had to do. So, the police had found some bones, so what, they couldn't pin anything on her or Walter; it would remain a mystery just as Ailbe's disappearance had been a mystery all those years ago. But she was now fixated on getting rid of Jenny. Then they could buy that property for Simon, and he could set up his own wine-making business. Alana had tuned out to be a sweet girl and Clare had made it up with her son. Life would be good again.

Clare returned to her apothecary and retrieved the syringes she had prepared earlier, and then retraced her steps back to the kitchen where she lovingly injected each cupcake with tincture of aconite. It was a large dose and they should all die almost immediately and feel no pain. It was a shame about Matt, he had been a loving nephew and she would miss him, but he clearly had designs on that English bitch. He had made his own bed.

Mission accomplished she placed a lace paper doily on one of her best cream ware plates and arranged the cakes attractively on top. They looked good enough to eat she laughed to herself. Then she transferred the whole to the interior of the plastic box and closed the lid with a satisfying snap. Returning to her apothecary to dispose of the syringes, she eyed the cupcake Matt had placed for her on the side – she would really enjoy that later she thought smugly.

On finishing helping his uncle with the fencing, Matt had showered and changed into smart jeans and a short sleeved pale blue shirt. Then he went downstairs to collect the cakes, just in time to see Aurum up on his hind legs, front paws splayed on the worktop, with his nose deep in the cake he had left for Clare. "Bad dog," yelled Matt, brushing the disobedient animal away. Aurum had managed to make quite a mess of the icing. Shame to waste it Matt thought and fed the greedy dog the spoiled cake, telling him he didn't deserve it, but giving him a friendly pat all the same. Matt then opened the box and replaced the empty space on the plate with a cake from the box. Then he got in his car and made his way down to Jenny's bearing his prize – he couldn't wait for them all to taste what was his first effort at baking.

Victoria had fetched the glasses to serve the wine. You need a small white wine glass Jenny she had said, to fully appreciate the wines honeyed nuances. She had asked Matt what time he was going to arrive so that she could take the bottle out of the fridge. It needed to be chilled, but not so cold as to obscure the subtle characteristics of the wine. Now, on Matt's arrival she rushed to open it. The two men greeted each other warmly. After that initial hazardous start things could have gone either way, but they liked each other's company and were getting on really well, much to my relief.

Matt had told me that he would bring something to accompany

the Sauternes, but in my wildest dreams I never imagined that he would actually make something himself.

"Look at these beauties, made with my own fair hand," said Matt with pride, as he opened the box and the sweet lemony smell of the cupcakes filled our nostrils tantalizingly.

"Just a moment Matt," Victoria said stridently. "You mean to say that you made these in Clare's kitchen?" Matt nodded, clearly perplexed.

"Did you have sight of them at all times?" Victoria continued, "You must have left them alone when you changed?"

Matt told us how he had made the cakes but gone to help his uncle and that Clare had put them in the box for him.

"Right," said Victoria determinedly, and to all our utter amazement she took the box from an astonished Matt, bore it into the kitchen, and emptied the whole lot into the bin.

"Just as well I made a tart au citron as a back-up," she said, brushing a hair away from her face.

Clare had finished her work in her apothecary for the day, and safely disposed of the syringes. Walter was still in the fields sorting out something or other, and now it was time to reward her efforts with a cup of coffee and that cupcake. She hummed contentedly to herself as she put the kettle on and fetched her favourite bone china cup and saucer, all the while looking at the cake bathed in its glistening, opulent icing. Finally, the water had boiled, and she poured it onto the coffee in the cafetière. This was an occasion for proper coffee she thought, none of that instant stuff. This was from that swanky coffee shop in Auckland, and its fruity, slightly caramelised aroma was blissful. Impatiently waiting the recommended four minutes, drumming her fingers on the worktop, her head was filled with images of the future she had planned out. Alana was certainly a stunning girl and astute too. She would give Walter and her beautiful, intelligent grandchildren, and everything would be just perfect.

Finally, the coffee was ready, and Clare poured it into the waiting cup with magisterial ceremony. Then she glided into the lounge holding the coffee in one hand and the cake in the other and sat down in her comfy Queen Anne wingback chair, putting her feet up on the matching footstool. She took a sip of the aromatic coffee, and then put the cup down on the adjacent mahogany side table. Sighing contentedly, she took a deep, gleeful bite into the moist cake, catching a glimpse of something fluttering through the open window as she did so. Two butterflies were chasing each other playfully in and out of the window, a Southern Blue, and a Small White. But wait, a third had appeared to join the joyful unit. It was one that Clare couldn't identify, but to her horror she saw that its colouring was black and yellow. A wave of sheer terror enveloped her. She tried to stand up, dropping the cake and knocking over the coffee table in the process. A pool of dark brown coffee spread over the polished parquet floor. She slumped back down in the chair again just as the black and yellow butterfly came to rest on her hand. It was the last thing she saw before darkness encircled her.

Victoria and Augustus had moved into the rented property down the road, and whilst he was busy with architect's designs, she was up with me by 9am every morning. We usually started the day with a catch-up over coffee on the verandah before she disappeared into the winery. But today we were going to taste the wine from the barrel. Although Victoria had tasted it regularly and would continue to do so during different stages of its development, she wanted now to share that experience with me. The wine had been in barrel for a month. It was still very young, but it would give us an idea of what the finished wine should be like, Victoria said.

"It will make your lips pucker Jenny, because the tannins won't have softened out yet, but this is an organoleptic educational experience," she announced, brandishing her wine thief; the pipette that wine-makers used to draw samples from barrels for the purpose of tasting developing wine.

Victoria told me that we would be evaluating the colour, aroma, flavour, texture, and nuances of the wine, as she uncorked the barrel, and dipped the thief into its inky depths to extract a sample.

She dribbled this into the waiting glasses that I held in anticipating hands.

"Everything is magnified 10-fold whilst wine is in barrel Jenny," said Victoria. "Try to look past the initial tannins and aim to identify the fruit and floral components underneath it all. Everything should be in proportion with each other, it's all about balance. There shouldn't be a strong oak element in this wine at any rate because the barrels are old, but I will invest in some new ones for our next vintage."

To me the wine tasted astringent and harsh, but Victoria assured me that astringency and rough tannins tell us that the wine will age well.

"Of course, it's too immature now, but wow will it be good in a few months' time. Underneath all that tannin is a refined gem!"

As we returned to the house to reward ourselves with a mug of coffee and a slice of the fruit cake I had made yesterday, Victoria declared that we would repeat this process every month now. I was elated, I had experienced a window into the future of our business, and I felt like I knew the personality of our wine.

We were lounging on the rattan chairs indulging in the coffee and cake when Matt and Augustus pulled up outside in Matt's car. The two men had become firm friends, sharing the same sense of humour and a love of sport. Matt had given Augustus a lift into town for a meeting he had with the architects. Now the two of them came towards us gossiping easily away like an old couple who had known each other for years.

"You two look like you've been up to no good," I said, smiling broadly. Augustus brought us up to speed on the house, and Matt told us about some new policies he was introducing to his practice.

I was just about to tell them about the barrel tasting session when Chief Inspector Peter Carter's car turned into the drive and parked up alongside Matt's.

"Coffee," I yelled as he got out of the car.

"Oh yes please," he answered, coming up the steps of the verandah with two butterflies, one white and one blue circling through the air in a frenzied dance above his head.

Peter took one of the rattan chairs as I fetched him a mug and a slice of cake, then settled back down to hear his news.

"Sorry to hear about your auntie," Peter said with sincerity, nodding to Matt. "Your dad let me know. How is Walter coping?"

"Uncle's never been one to show his emotions too much," replied Matt. "He found her dead you know, in her wingback chair, and it was a shock because she hadn't been ill. We knew she had a heart problem though, and apparently she had a massive heart attack. Uncle doesn't want a post-mortem, he says that Clare wouldn't have wanted that, and as there weren't any suspicious circumstances it isn't necessary. I'm staying with him at the moment, at least until the funeral is over anyway. Simon is a great help and Alana is sending up more home-made food than we can eat, so uncle has a lot of support."

"That's good to know," said Peter, "but the reason for my visit is that I've come to update you on the case," he cleared his throat. "Unfortunately we haven't been able to find out who killed the animals and left the notes, and as there hasn't been a repeat of any of that, I'm sorry to have to inform you that we're closing our investigations," he said, sinking even white teeth eagerly into the cake.

"Great cake," he mumbled with his mouth full. Once he'd swallowed, he continued, "We can assume from the DNA testing, and the charm bracelet she always wore, that one set of bones is Ailbe, and the other is a miscarried infant of Amelia and Horace's. Amelia's sister is going to give both infants a proper burial."

"When is that going to take place?" I inquired. Peter took a gulp of his coffee and glanced at his watch.

"Well actually about now," he replied. "The sister arranged for the remains to be interred with Amelia, since she was the mother of both infants."

The butterflies continued their dance, less hectic now, and eventually came to rest on the rail of the verandah. They were facing each other with their antennae touching; they looked like they were kissing.

"How exquisitely beautiful they are, so other worldly," I breathed, and with that they raced off towards the vines, and seemed to disappear, melting into the air.

I didn't notice a third butterfly had appeared on the scene, an

Australian Painted lady. This one didn't come to rest on the rail, but darted around fitfully at a distance, as if it were searching for something that only it could see.

I felt a peaceful embrace come over me, and although I couldn't pin the feeling down, I somehow knew that it was the dawning of a new era.

Eight months later.

It was the beginning of summer and Victoria and I watched from the verandah, coffee mugs in hand, as another consignment of bricks arrived. The foundations were nearly finished now, and you could see the outline of the house, and the floor plan of where the downstairs rooms would be. There was going to be a huge bi-fold window at the back overlooking the valley and the vines. Augustus waved a cheery hand at us, and then returned to a confab with the builders.

"I'm so glad you two were able to work it out," I told Victoria, turning to meet her beaming smile. She had never looked so radiant.

"Funny how things turn out isn't it Jenny," she mused. "Who would have thought a year ago that we would both be standing here looking at that view, it really is breathtaking," she said, waving her arm at the vista before us.

It was a glorious day and the roses were in bloom at the edge of the vines. Victoria had explained to me how rose bushes were historically planted at the end of rows because they were susceptible to the same diseases as the vines but showed signs of infection earlier. So, they were a means of early detection, allowing you to take the necessary precautions. But these days with modern viticultural methods enabling you to monitor things more scientifically, it was no longer strictly necessary to plant them. Now roses were more for aesthetic purposes, and a link with the past, creating a sense of nostalgia.

There was no denying that the vineyard looked stunning. We had planted an assortment of rose bushes intermittently at the end of the rows but chosen a white "Boule de Neige" and a blue "Blue for You" to plant where the bones had been found.

Taking a walk down to the spot, we each bent our heads to smell the heady fragrance of the flowers that were lifting their heads to the morning sun, releasing their scent into the still air. We noted that we hadn't seen the white and blue butterflies that used to be a regular sight on the vineyard for some time, but an Australian Painted Lady was often to be seen flying jerkily around like it was looking for somewhere to go, but didn't know the way.

The grapes were coming along fine, the flowers had set.

"It's going to be a bumper harvest," said Victoria, fingering one of the inconsequential hard green clusters that would in time evolve into a bunch of juicy black grapes.

"Thank goodness," I replied with a grin. "We are fast running out of wine to sell."

The last few months had been magical, and I had become something of a local celebrity. We had won second prize at the Annual New Zealand Wine Show with our pinot noir.

"It'll be first next year," Victoria had declared, but we were both delighted with the outcome. The vineyard was open to the public at weekends, and most Saturdays and Sundays were busy with people driving up from Auckland, and often much further afield, wanting to taste our wine and vermouth. It was a rare occurrence indeed if they didn't leave with a few bottles. A local restaurant had even stocked the wine, and Victoria was in negotiations with a company in London for a cocktail bar in Mayfair to take our vermouth.

Victoria and I were both in deep discussion about this when a yell from the postman interrupted our exchange.

"Got a parcel for you Jenny that needs to be signed for," he shouted. I knew what it was; Victoria had persuaded me to take the WSET certificates.

"When someone asks you what your wine tastes like, you just can't keep saying 'very nice' Jenny," she had told me like an old schoolmarm. But I knew she was right, and I had already completed the Level 1 certificate gaining a distinction. I was over the moon, but I think Victoria was even more thrilled with my achievement than I was. Now the Level 2 book and accompanying documentation had arrived. It would be quite a step up from the first level Victoria had told me, but that I was going to get another distinction.

"No pressure then," I joked as I signed for the parcel with a satisfied flourish.

Just then the sky started to cloud over, and a slight drizzle of rain began to fall, making wet splats on the paper of the parcel. Hastily thanking the postie Victoria and I darted up the steps of the verandah and under the safety of its tin roof just as the heavens opened.

"Only a shower I think," Victoria said, then seeing Augustus running up from the building site, and the builders dashing into the winery for cover, "I'll get the coffee on."

By the time Augustus reached me he was drenched.

"Make a cup for the lads would you Vix," he shouted to the direction of the kitchen.

"Already on it," Victoria's chirpy reply came from within.

"Better make an extra mug," I chipped in, "Matt's just arrived." Augustus shouted a greeting to Matt and disappeared into the house to help his wife.

Matt had told us that Walter had handed over the farm to Simon, and would remain living there, but Simon and Alana had moved in to run it. Alana was four months pregnant. They had only just announced the pregnancy, wanting to wait until the first crucial three months were over. Now that they knew everything was as it should be they had announced to the community that the scan had revealed that Alana was expecting twins, a boy and a girl. Walter couldn't have been happier.

Matt always stayed with his uncle when he came down, and Walter had definitely changed since Clare's death. He was somehow more relaxed, more open and easy-going.

I went out onto the verandah to meet Matt. The rain had started to ease off. It had only been a shower after all, but his dark hair was glistening with raindrops shining in the emerging sunshine. He was carrying a cardboard box, with the top loosely closed.

"What's in there?" I inquired looking up at his handsome face.

"Why don't you take a look?" he replied with an enigmatic smile, placing the box on one of the rattan chairs.

Reaching down, I gingerly parted the flaps of the box and squealed in delight. Inside was the most beautiful jet-black kitten with bright blue eyes.

"Oh, thank you, thank you," I shrieked, flinging my arms round Matt's neck. I held him close in a tight hug, and then I pulled away to plant a resounding kiss on his cheek.

"It's a little girl," said Matt, beaming with delight.

I bent down and scooped the mewing bundle into my hands and cuddled her into my shoulder, where she nuzzled contentedly.

"I love the way their eyes are always blue at birth, like most human babies," I mused, stroking the obsidian fur under the kitten's chin.

"This one's eyes won't change colour," began Matt, "She's a black Javanese. It took me a long time to source her," he continued, joining in stroking the kitten.

"What are you going to call her?"

"That's easy," I replied. The rain had completely ceased now, and the sky had returned to a clear bright blue, which mirrored both the kitten's eyes and my own. The most beautiful rainbow was arching over the valley, its seven glowing colours illuminated by the rays of the penetrating sun.

"Iris," I said, placing a tender kiss on his lips, "The goddess of the rainbow."

THE END

Printed in Great Britain
by Amazon